12/12

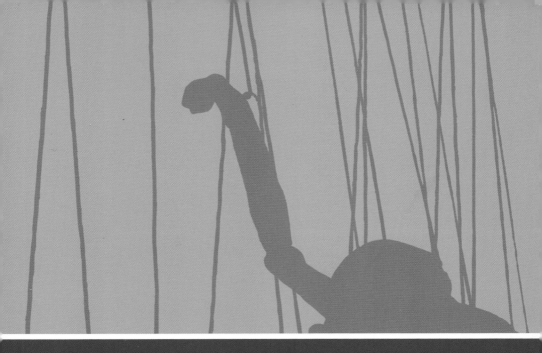

CARLO COLLODI'S

PINOCCHIO

STONE ARCH BOOKS
MINNEAPOLIS   SAN DIEGO

CARLO COLLODI'S

PINOCCHIO

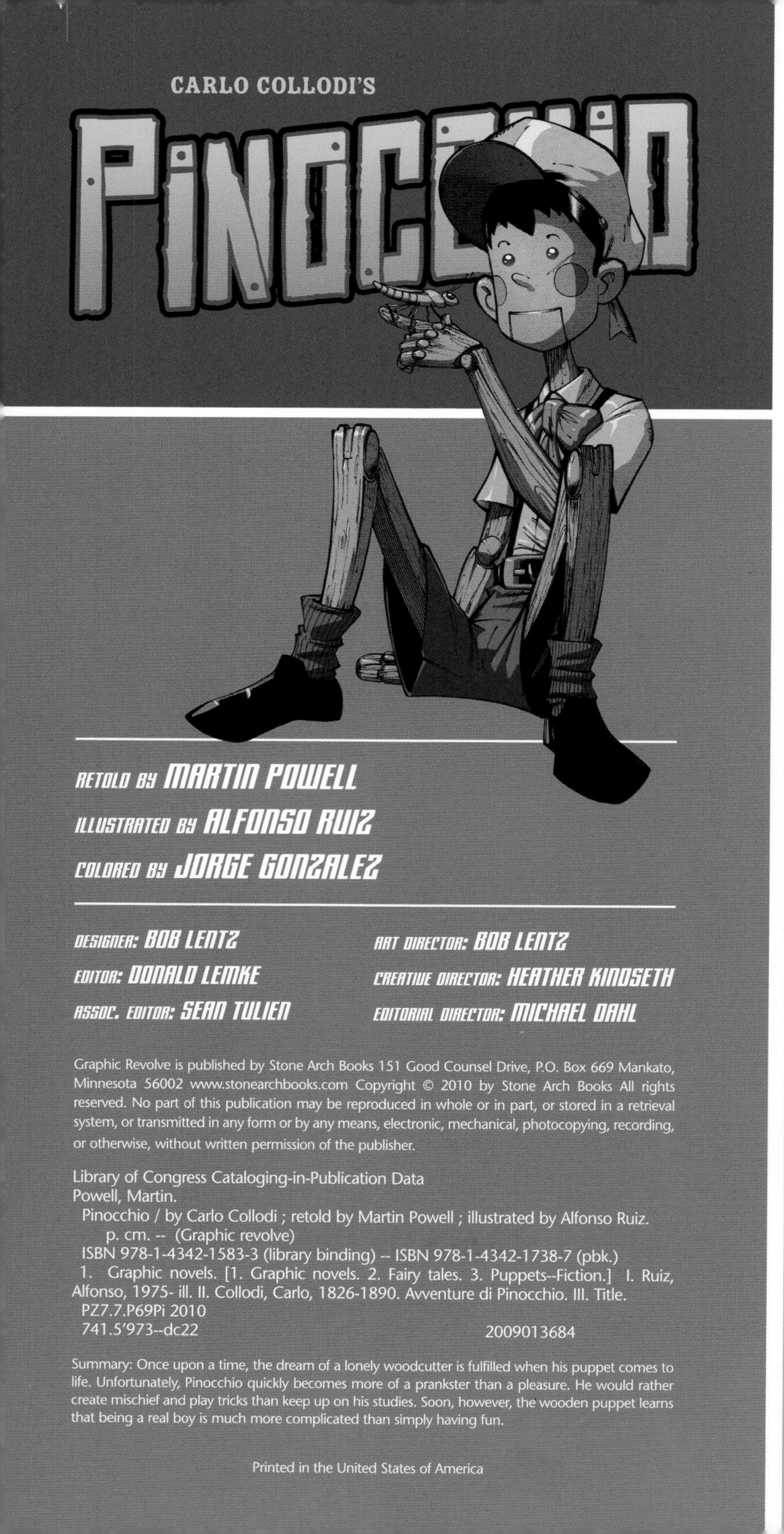

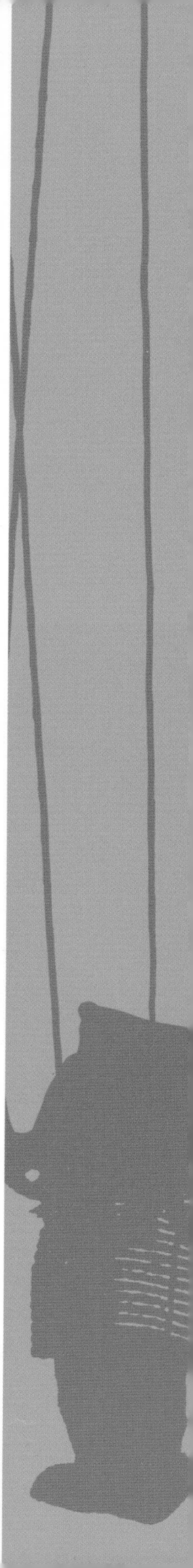

RETOLD BY MARTIN POWELL

ILLUSTRATED BY ALFONSO RUIZ

COLORED BY JORGE GONZALEZ

DESIGNER: BOB LENTZ

EDITOR: DONALD LEMKE

ASSOC. EDITOR: SEAN TULIEN

ART DIRECTOR: BOB LENTZ

CREATIVE DIRECTOR: HEATHER KINDSETH

EDITORIAL DIRECTOR: MICHAEL DAHL

Graphic Revolve is published by Stone Arch Books 151 Good Counsel Drive, P.O. Box 669 Mankato, Minnesota 56002 www.stonearchbooks.com

Library of Congress Cataloging-in-Publication Data
Powell, Martin.
Pinocchio / by Carlo Collodi ; retold by Martin Powell ; illustrated by Alfonso Ruiz.
p. cm. -- (Graphic revolve)
ISBN 978-1-4342-1583-3 (library binding) -- ISBN 978-1-4342-1738-7 (pbk.)
1. Graphic novels. [1. Graphic novels. 2. Fairy tales. 3. Puppets--Fiction.] I. Ruiz, Alfonso, 1975- ill. II. Collodi, Carlo, 1826-1890. Avventure di Pinocchio. III. Title.
PZ7.7.P69Pi 2010
741.5'973--dc22 2009013684

Summary: Once upon a time, the dream of a lonely woodcutter is fulfilled when his puppet comes to life. Unfortunately, Pinocchio quickly becomes more of a prankster than a pleasure. He would rather create mischief and play tricks than keep up on his studies. Soon, however, the wooden puppet learns that being a real boy is much more complicated than simply having fun.

Printed in the United States of America

CONTENTS

J-GN
PINOCCHIO
410-6848

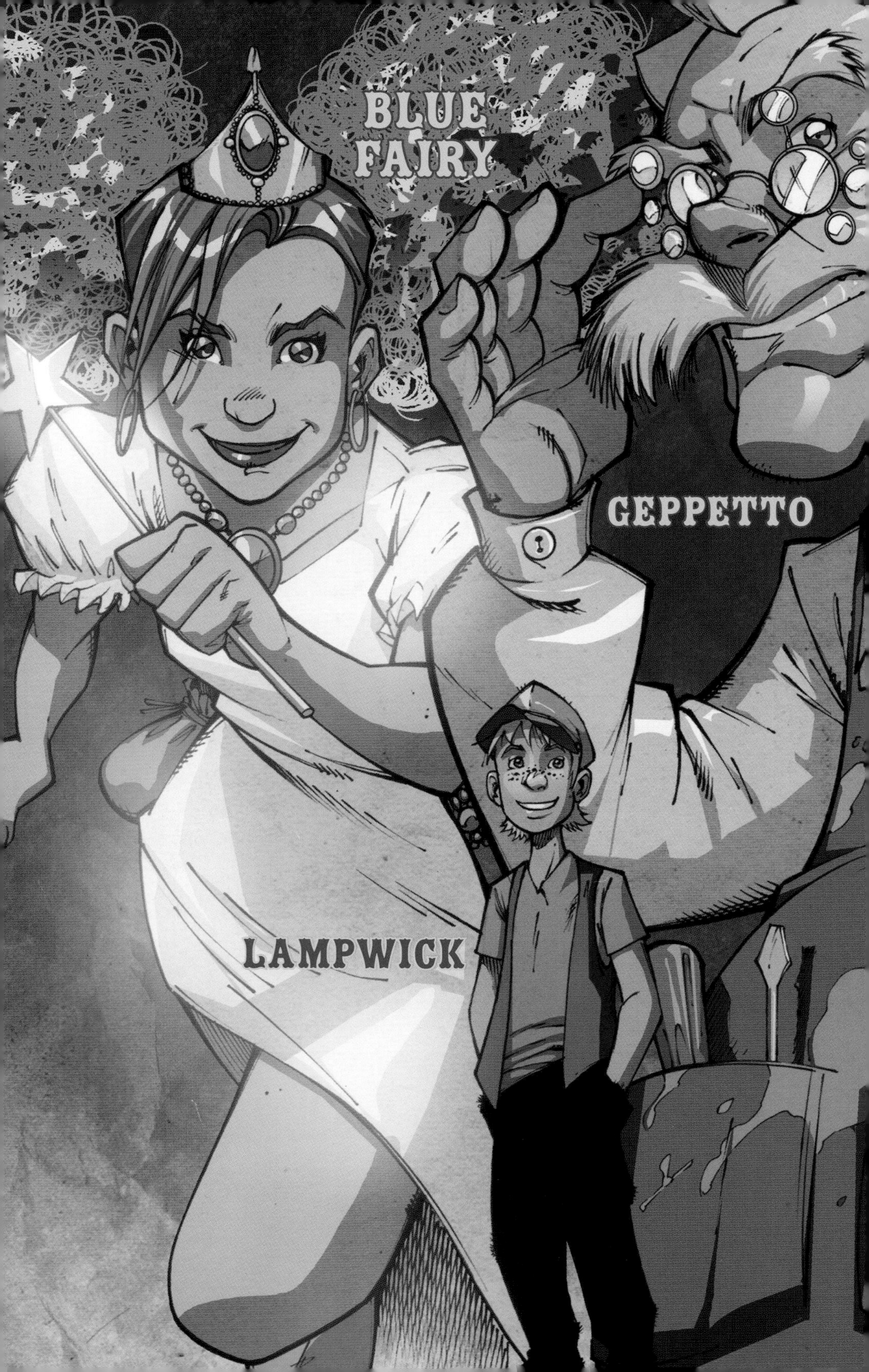
BLUE FAIRY
GEPPETTO
LAMPWICK

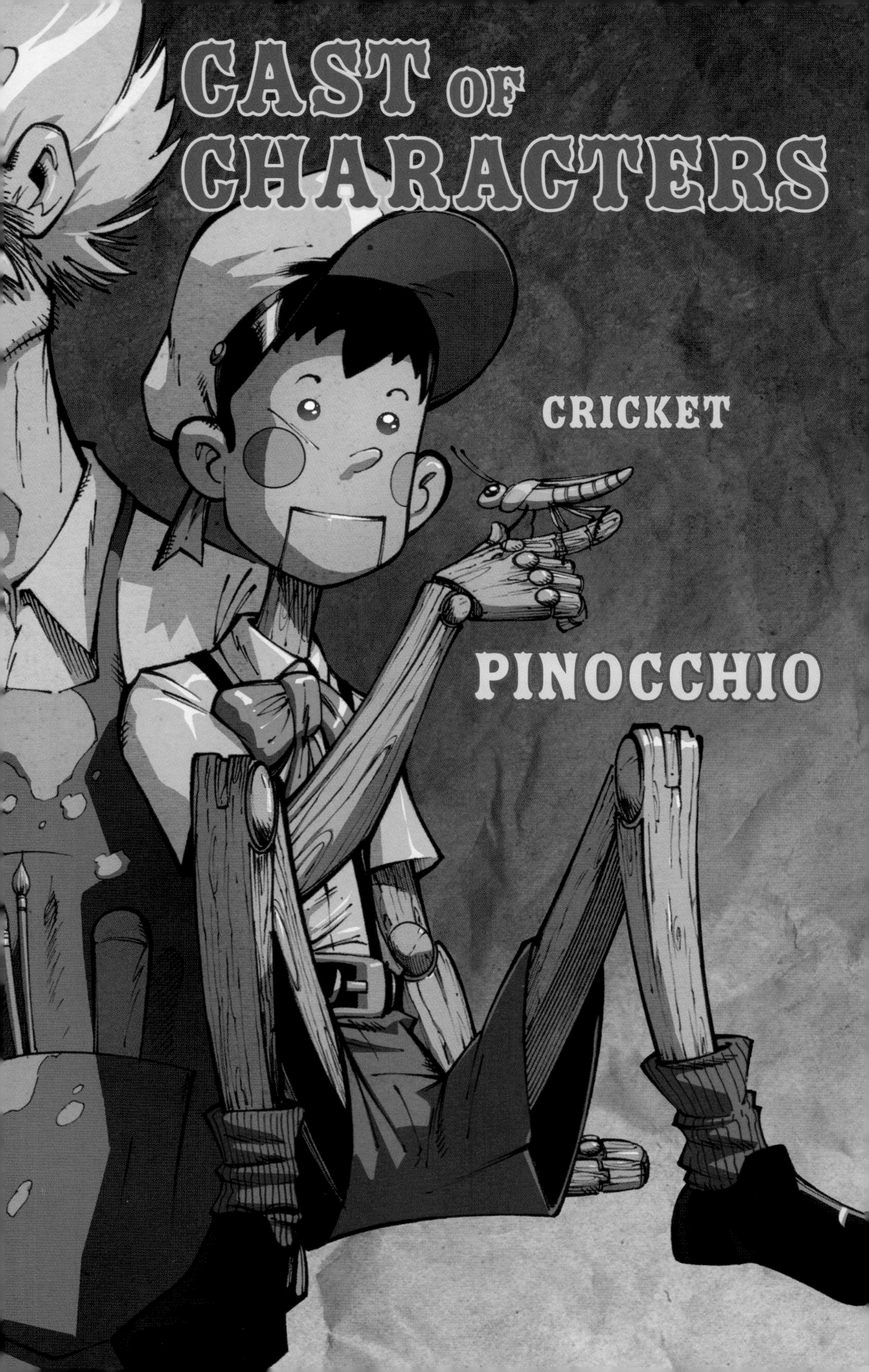
CAST OF CHARACTERS
CRICKET
PINOCCHIO

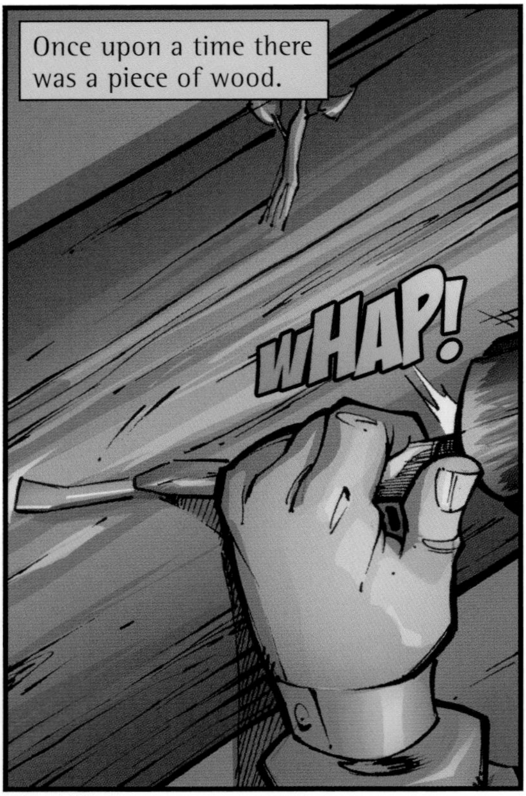
Once upon a time there was a piece of wood.
wHAP!

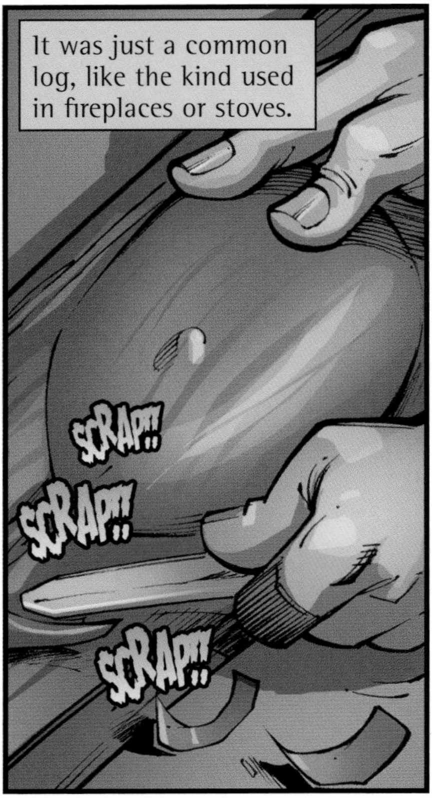
It was just a common log, like the kind used in fireplaces or stoves.
SCRAP!!
SCRAP!!
SCRAP!!

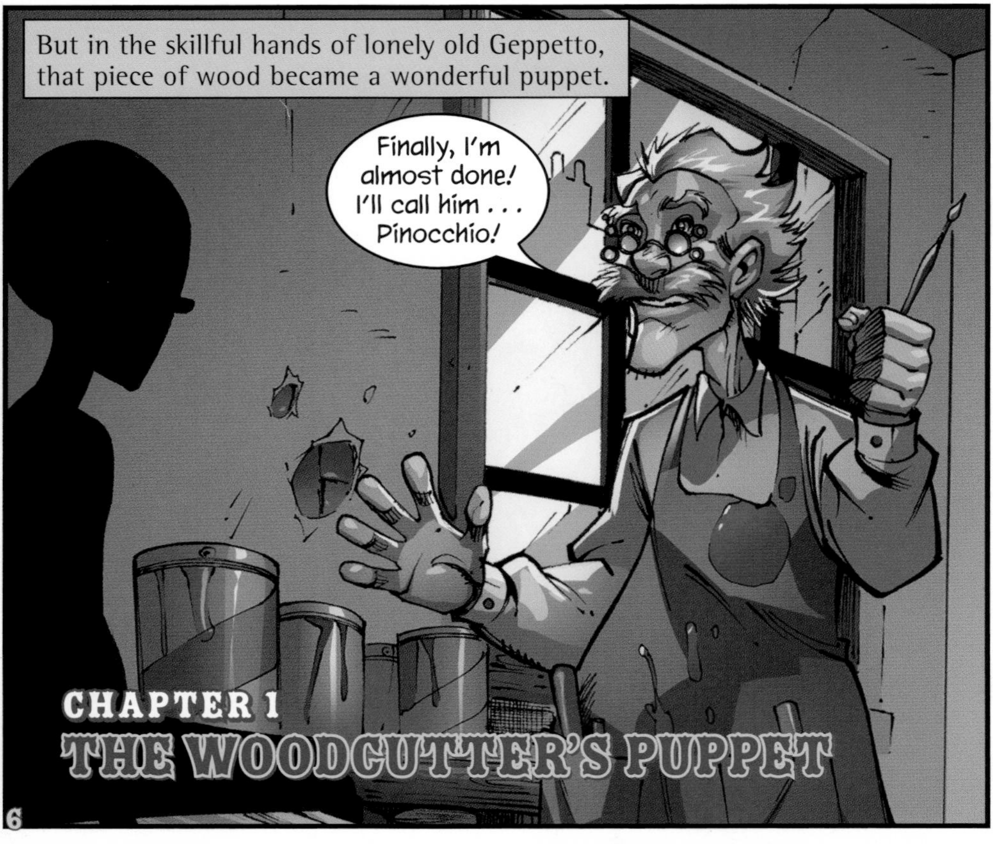
But in the skillful hands of lonely old Geppetto, that piece of wood became a wonderful puppet.
Finally, I'm almost done! I'll call him . . . Pinocchio!
CHAPTER 1
THE WOODCUTTER'S PUPPET

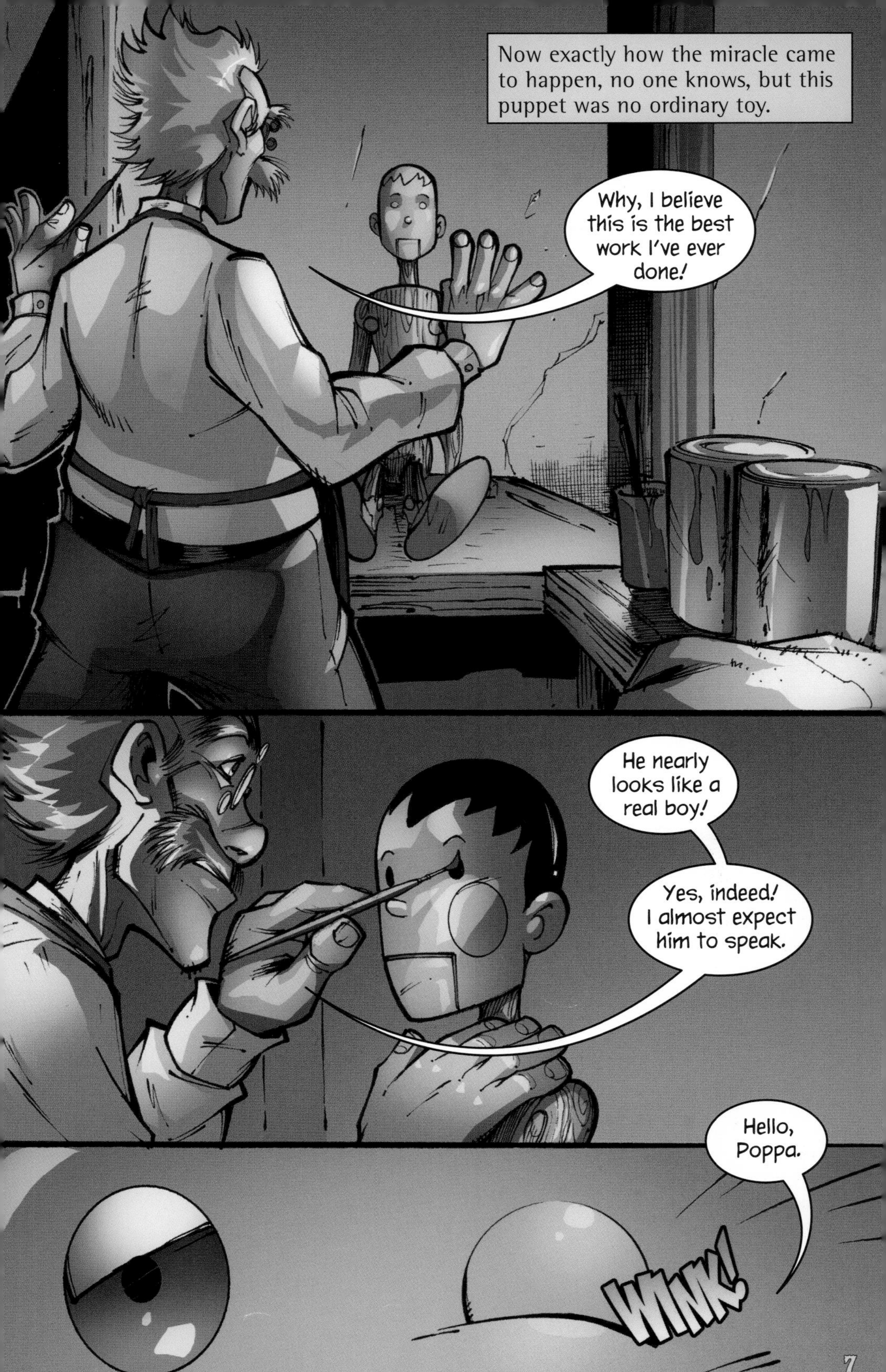
Now exactly how the miracle came to happen, no one knows, but this puppet was no ordinary toy.
Why, I believe this is the best work I've ever done!
He nearly looks like a real boy!
Yes, indeed! I almost expect him to speak.
Hello, Poppa.
WINK!

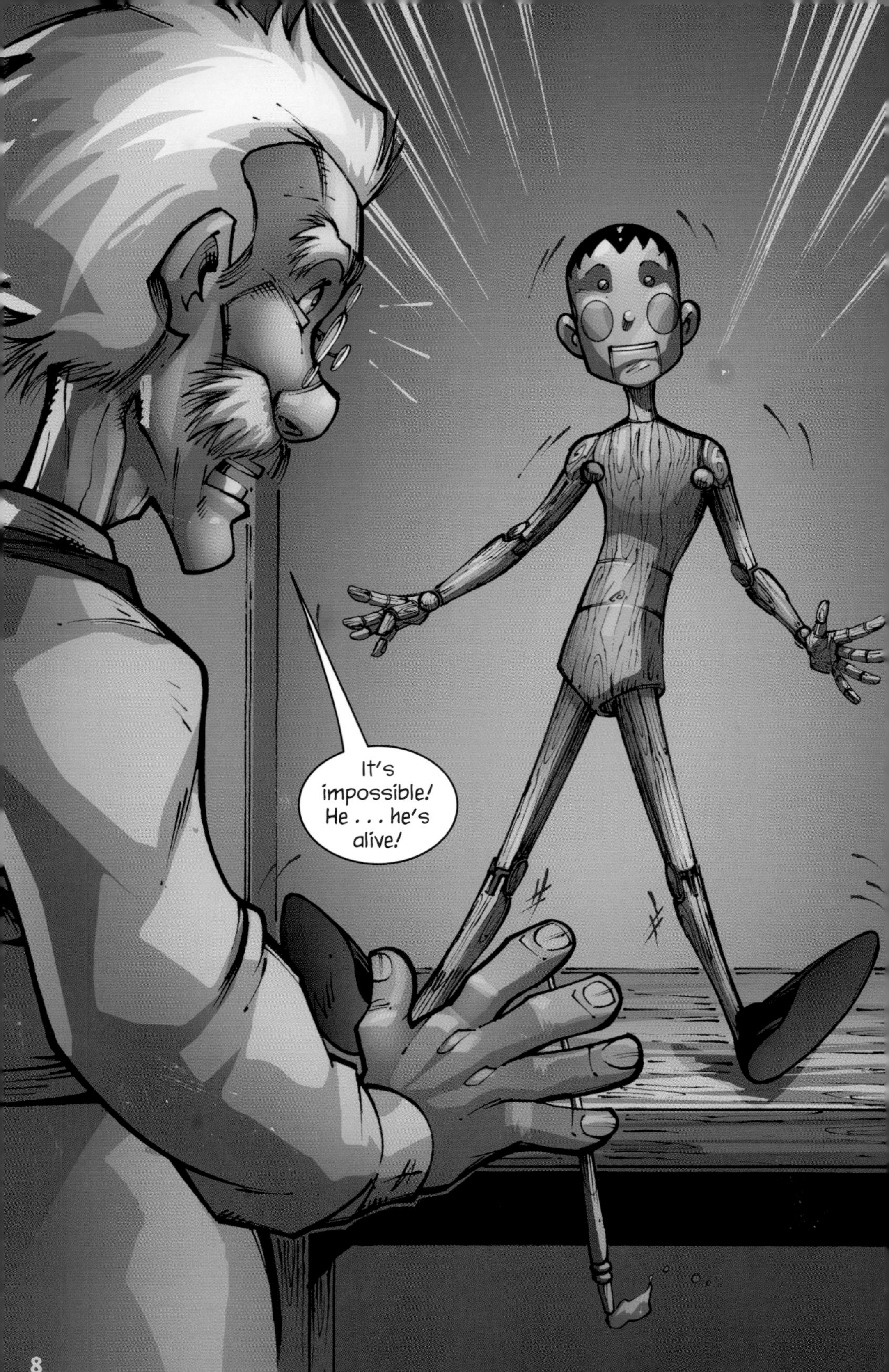
It's impossible! He . . . he's alive!

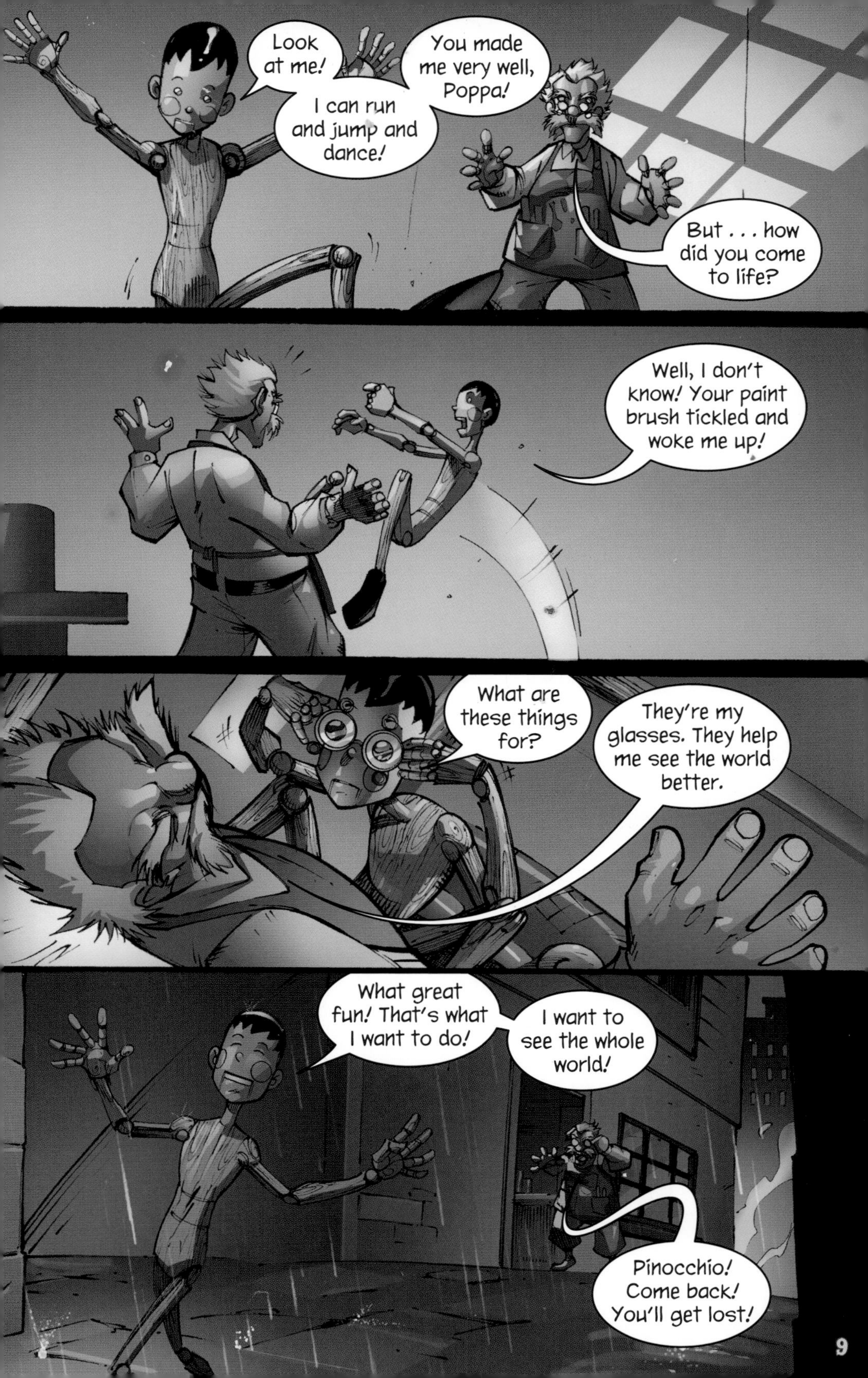
Look at me!
I can run and jump and dance!
You made me very well, Poppa!
But . . . how did you come to life?
Well, I don't know! Your paint brush tickled and woke me up!
What are these things for?
They're my glasses. They help me see the world better.
What great fun! That's what I want to do!
I want to see the whole world!
Pinocchio! Come back! You'll get lost!

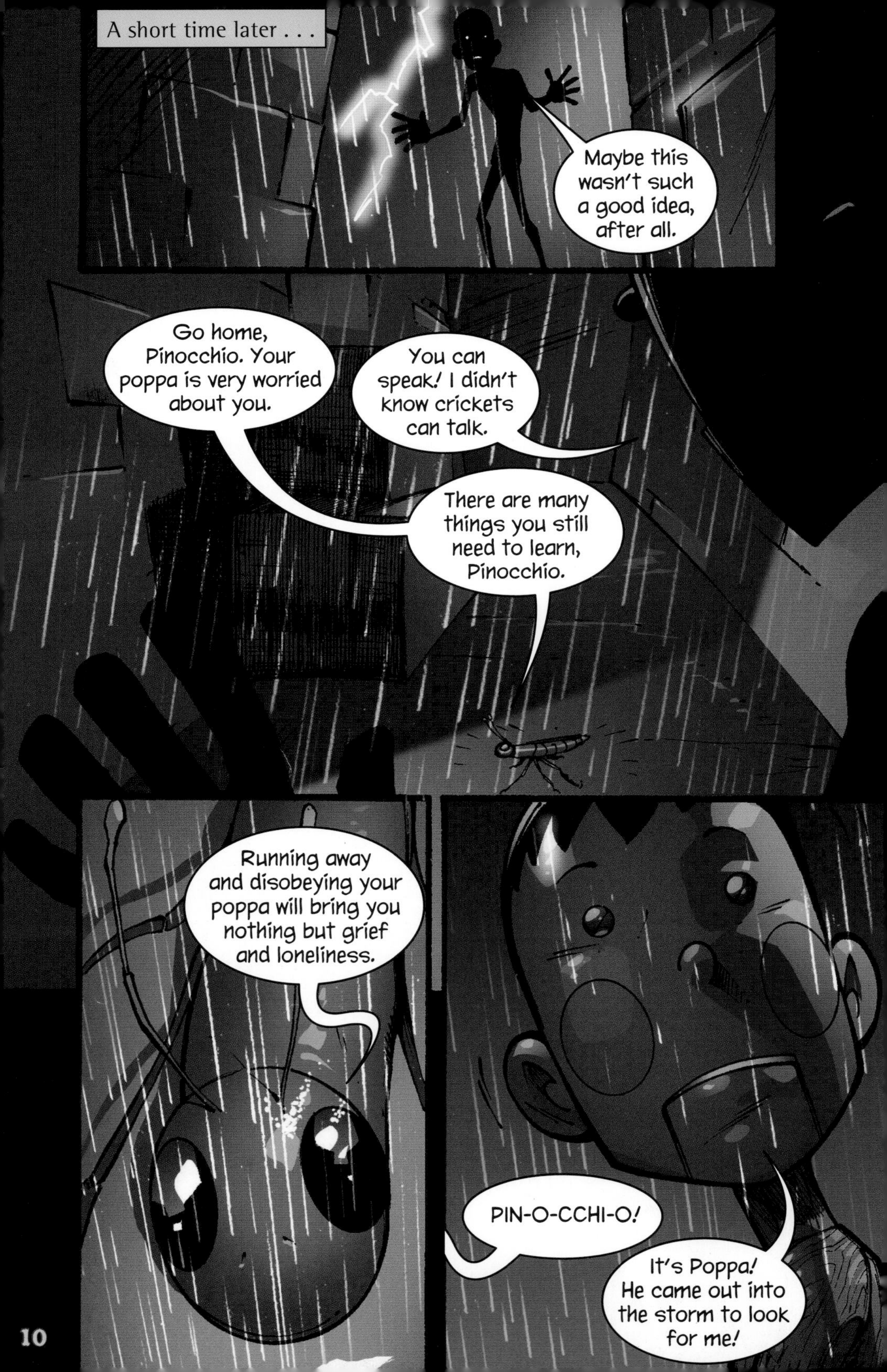
A short time later . . .
Maybe this wasn't such a good idea, after all.
Go home, Pinocchio. Your poppa is very worried about you.
You can speak! I didn't know crickets can talk.
There are many things you still need to learn, Pinocchio.
Running away and disobeying your poppa will bring you nothing but grief and loneliness.
PIN-O-CCHI-O!
It's Poppa! He came out into the storm to look for me!

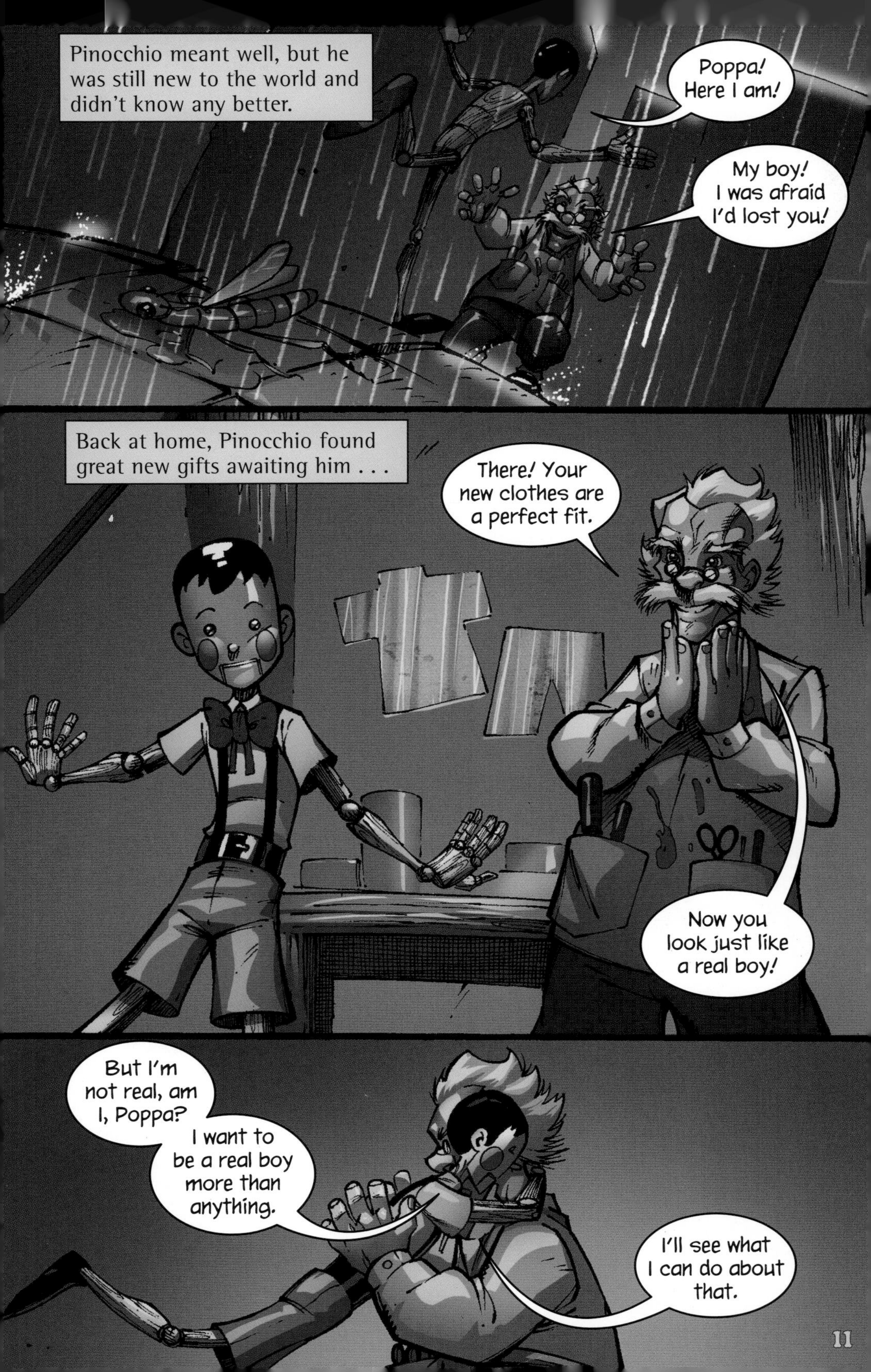
Pinocchio meant well, but he was still new to the world and didn't know any better.
Poppa! Here I am!
My boy! I was afraid I'd lost you!
Back at home, Pinocchio found great new gifts awaiting him . . .
There! Your new clothes are a perfect fit.
Now you look just like a real boy!
But I'm not real, am I, Poppa?
I want to be a real boy more than anything.
I'll see what I can do about that.

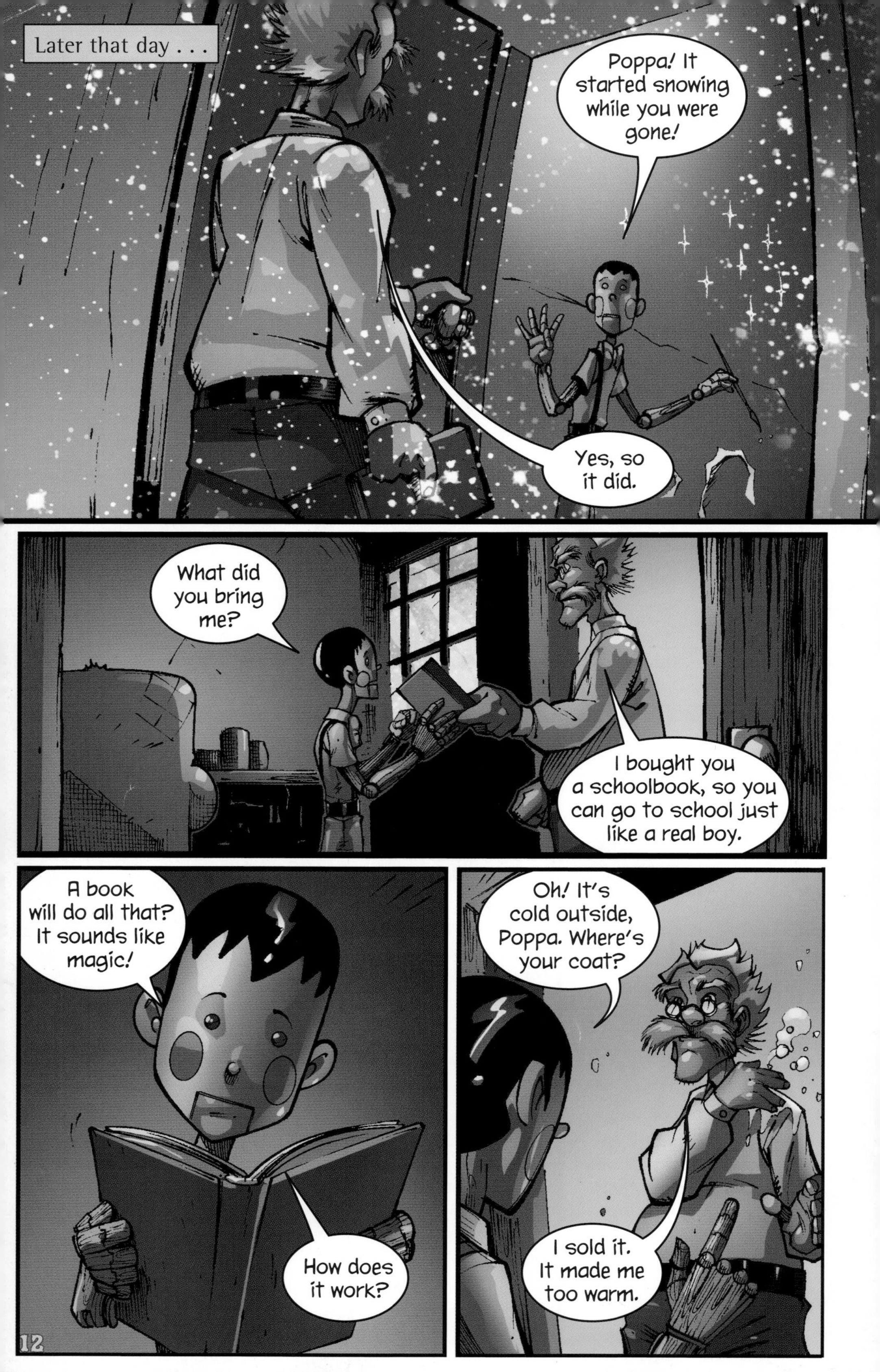
Later that day . . .
Poppa! It started snowing while you were gone!
Yes, so it did.
What did you bring me?
I bought you a schoolbook, so you can go to school just like a real boy.
A book will do all that? It sounds like magic!
How does it work?
Oh! It's cold outside, Poppa. Where's your coat?
I sold it. It made me too warm.

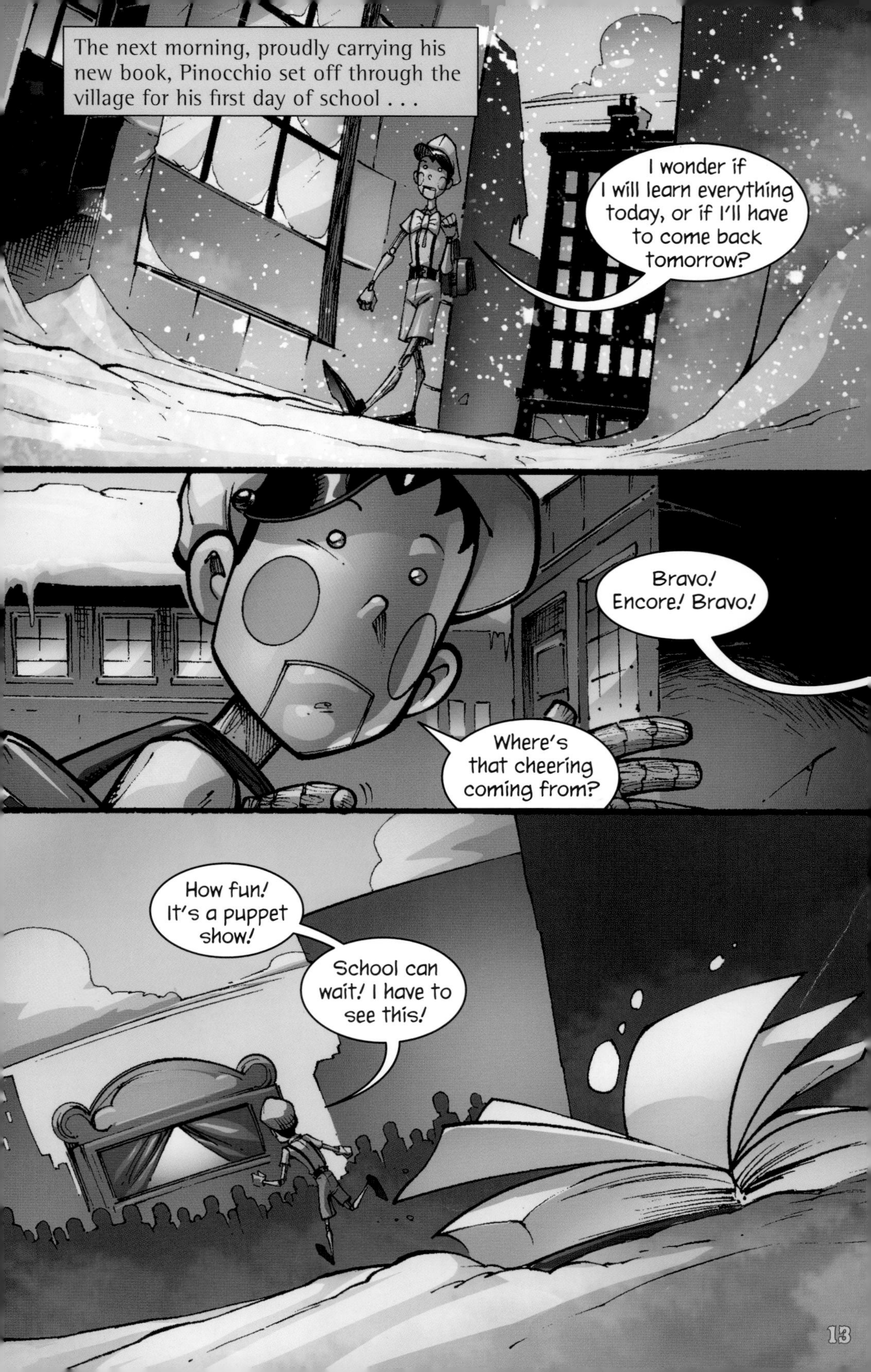

The next morning, proudly carrying his new book, Pinocchio set off through the village for his first day of school . . .
I wonder if I will learn everything today, or if I'll have to come back tomorrow?
Bravo! Encore! Bravo!
Where's that cheering coming from?
How fun! It's a puppet show!
School can wait! I have to see this!

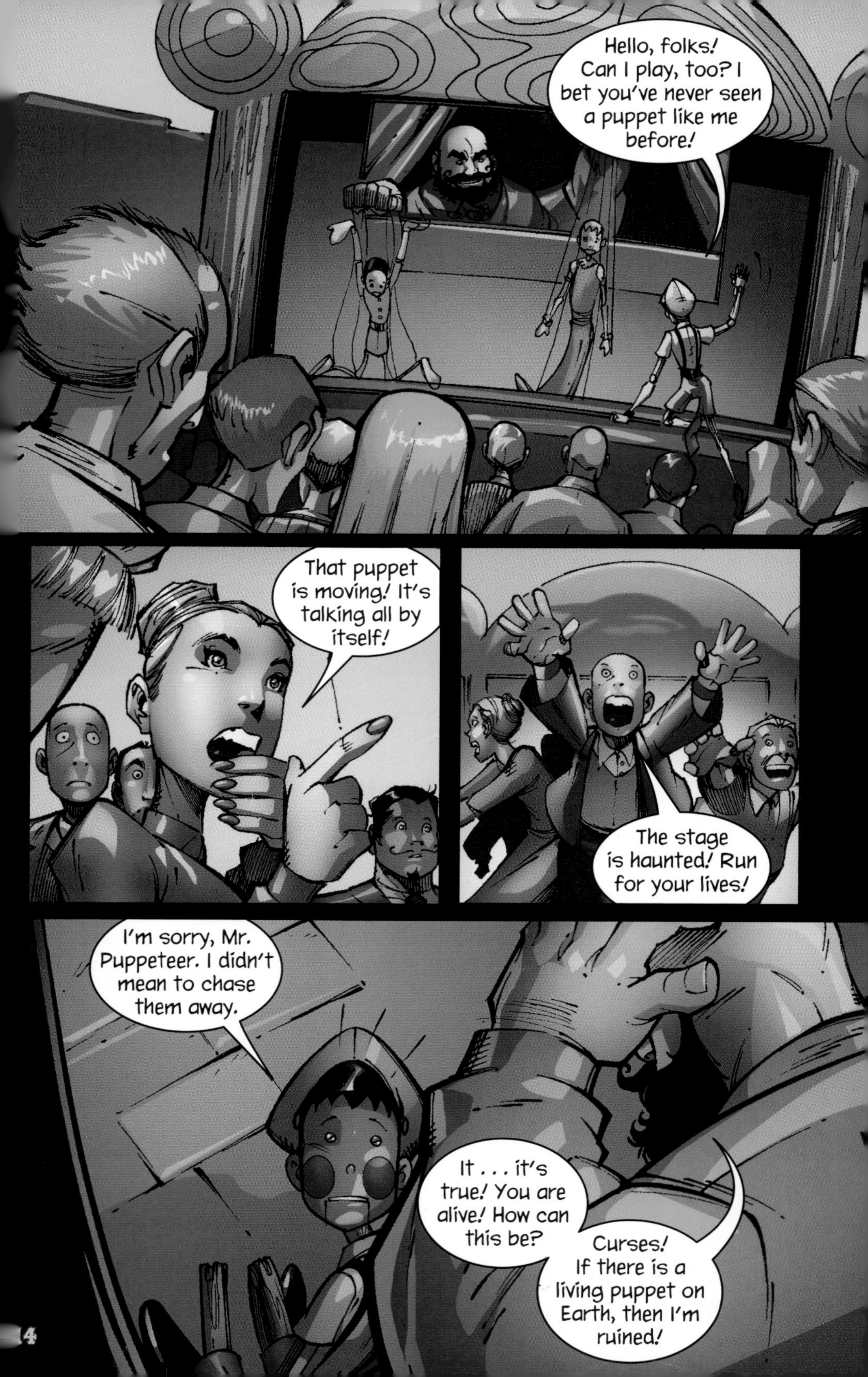
Hello, folks! Can I play, too? I bet you've never seen a puppet like me before!
That puppet is moving! It's talking all by itself!
The stage is haunted! Run for your lives!
I'm sorry, Mr. Puppeteer. I didn't mean to chase them away.
It . . . it's true! You are alive! How can this be?
Curses! If there is a living puppet on Earth, then I'm ruined!

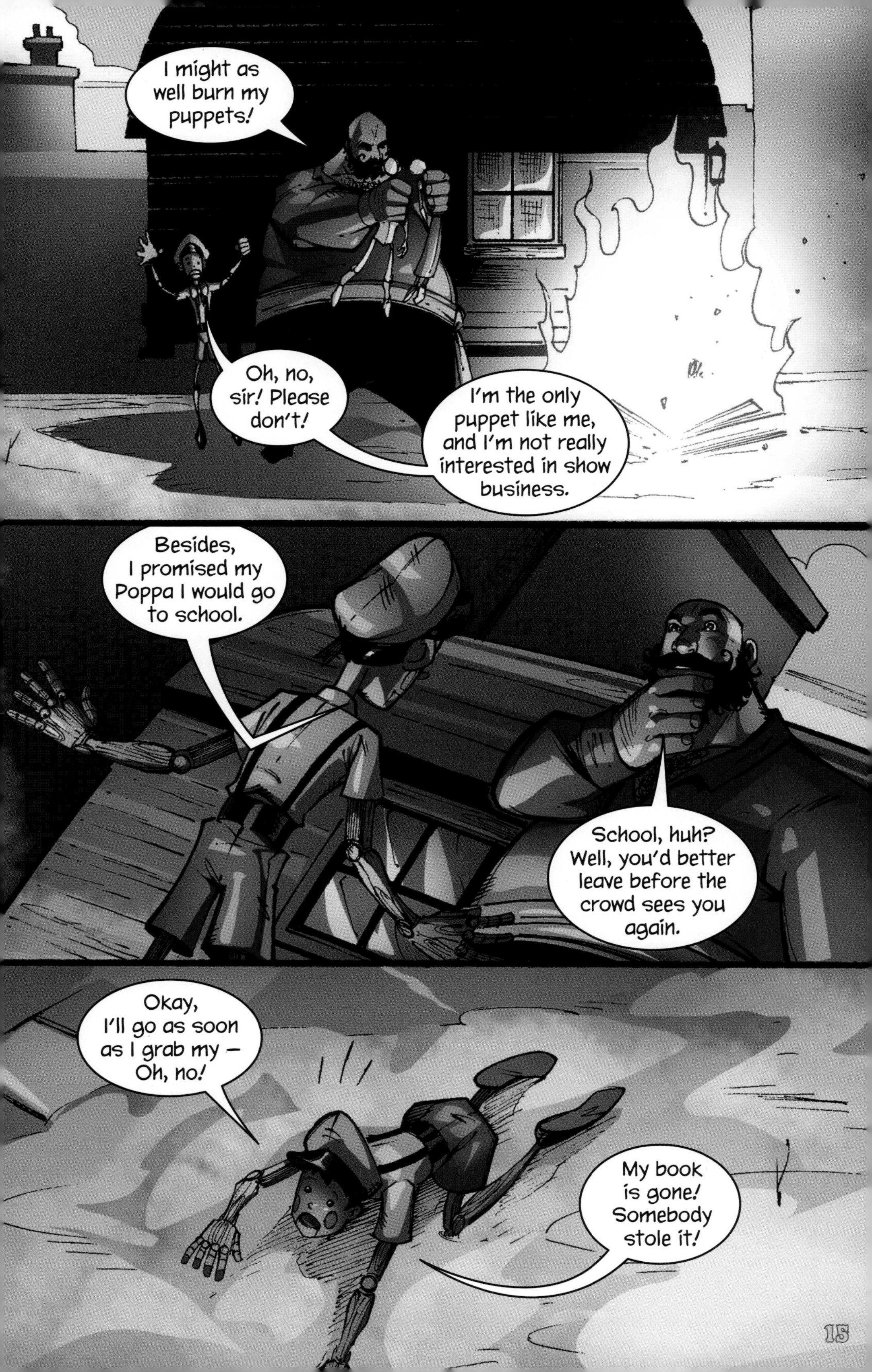
I might as well burn my puppets!
Oh, no, sir! Please don't!
I'm the only puppet like me, and I'm not really interested in show business.
Besides, I promised my Poppa I would go to school.
School, huh? Well, you'd better leave before the crowd sees you again.
Okay, I'll go as soon as I grab my — Oh, no!
My book is gone! Somebody stole it!

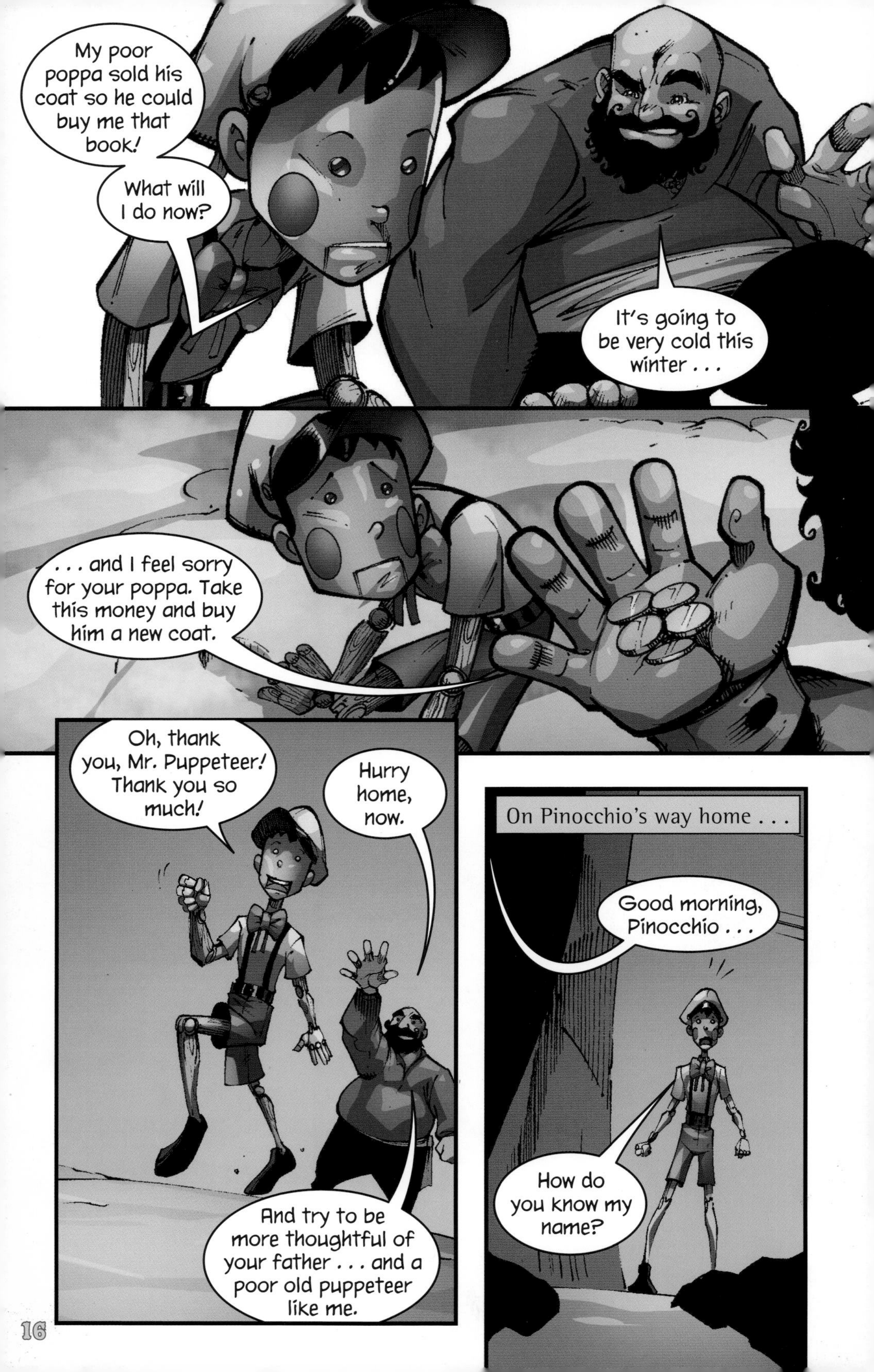
My poor poppa sold his coat so he could buy me that book!
What will I do now?
It's going to be very cold this winter . . .
. . . and I feel sorry for your poppa. Take this money and buy him a new coat.
Oh, thank you, Mr. Puppeteer! Thank you so much!
Hurry home, now.
And try to be more thoughtful of your father . . . and a poor old puppeteer like me.
On Pinocchio's way home . . .
Good morning, Pinocchio . . .
How do you know my name?

CHAPTER 2

MR. FOX AND MISS CAT

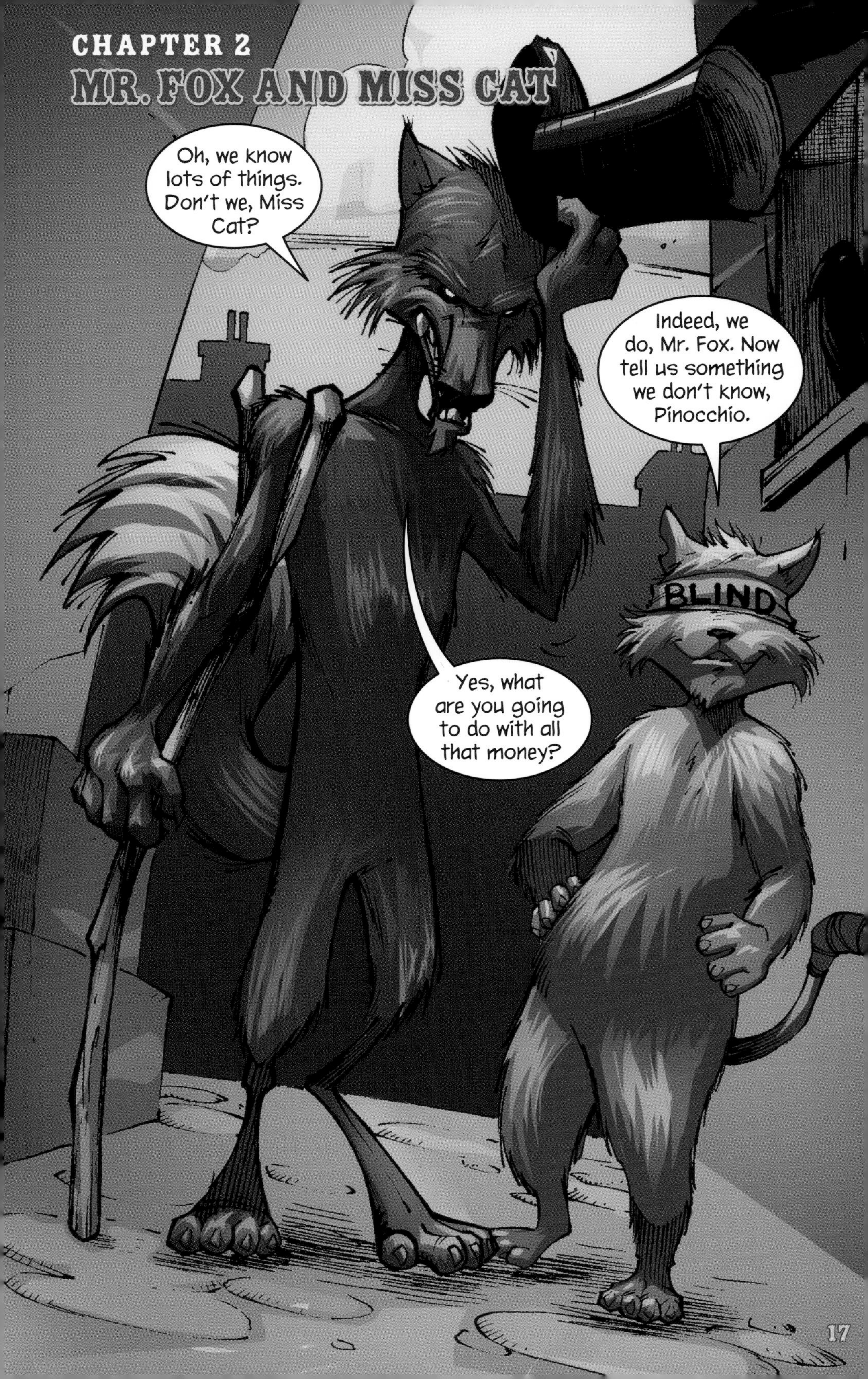

BLIND
Oh, we know lots of things. Don't we, Miss Cat?
Indeed, we do, Mr. Fox. Now tell us something we don't know, Pinocchio.
Yes, what are you going to do with all that money?

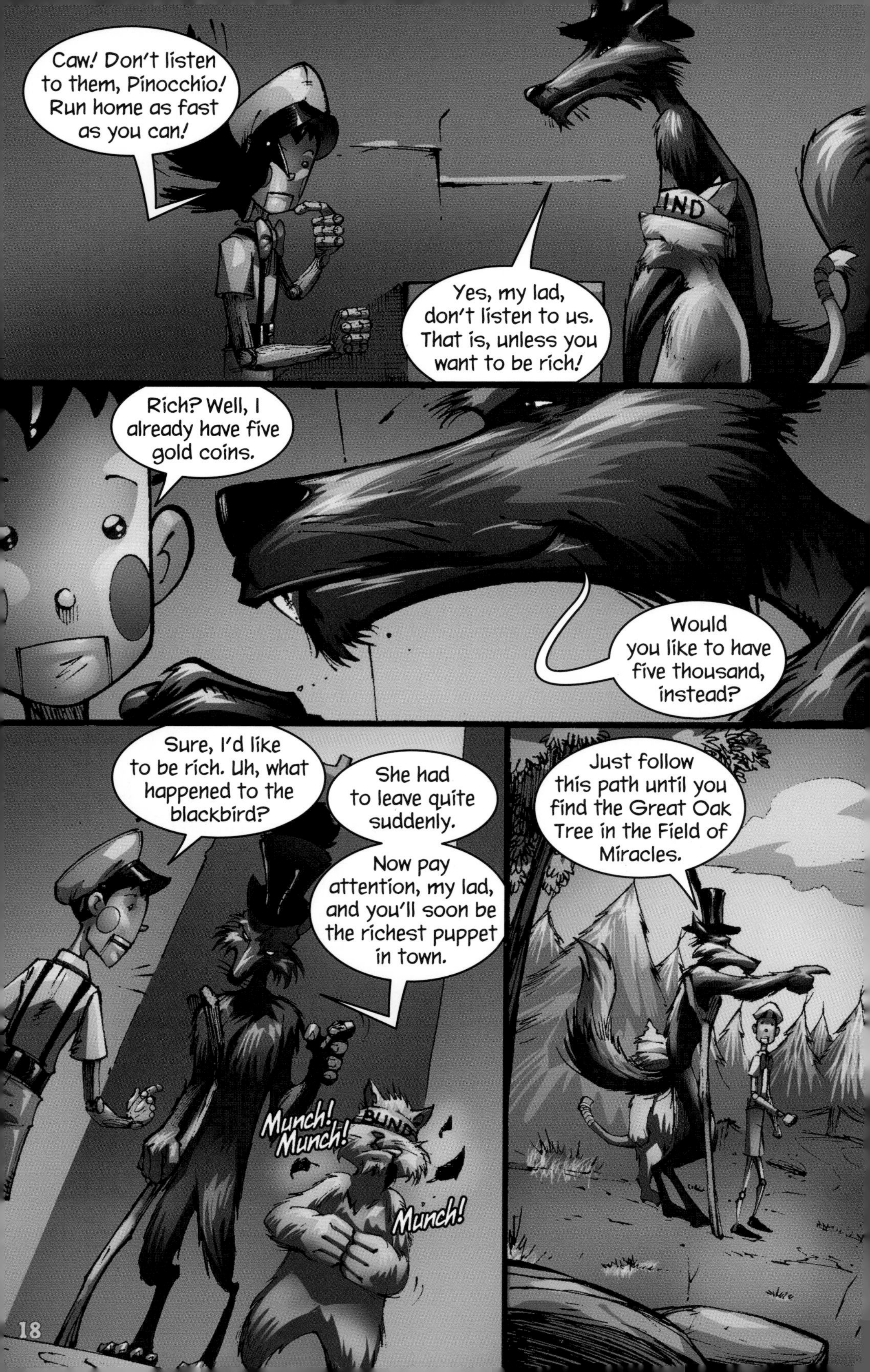

Caw! Don't listen to them, Pinocchio! Run home as fast as you can!
Yes, my lad, don't listen to us. That is, unless you want to be rich!
Rich? Well, I already have five gold coins.
Would you like to have five thousand, instead?
Sure, I'd like to be rich. Uh, what happened to the blackbird?
She had to leave quite suddenly.
Now pay attention, my lad, and you'll soon be the richest puppet in town.
Munch! Munch!
Munch!
Just follow this path until you find the Great Oak Tree in the Field of Miracles.

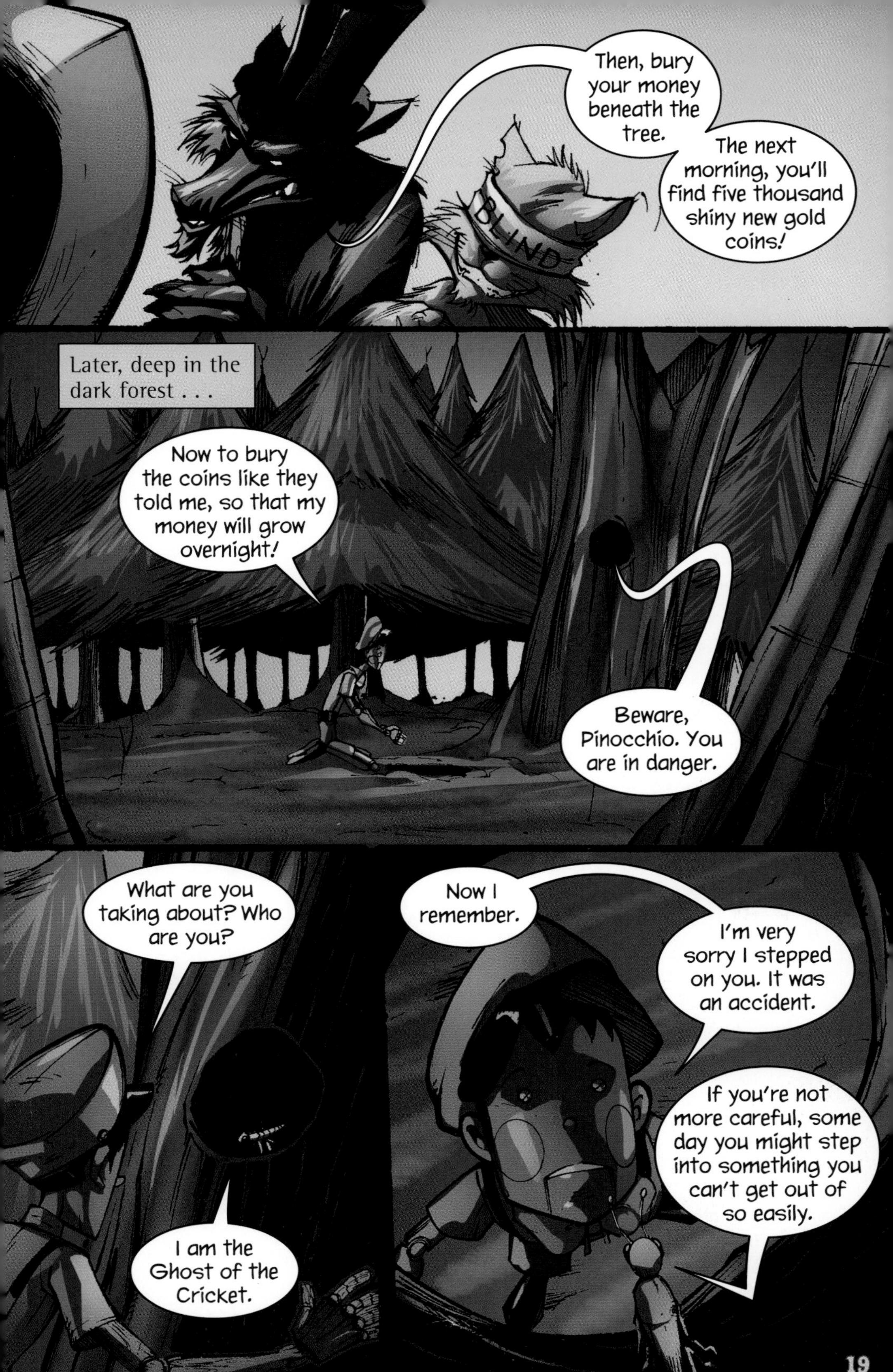
Then, bury your money beneath the tree.
The next morning, you'll find five thousand shiny new gold coins!
BLIND
Later, deep in the dark forest . . .
Now to bury the coins like they told me, so that my money will grow overnight!
Beware, Pinocchio. You are in danger.
What are you taking about? Who are you?
I am the Ghost of the Cricket.
Now I remember.
I'm very sorry I stepped on you. It was an accident.
If you're not more careful, some day you might step into something you can't get out of so easily.

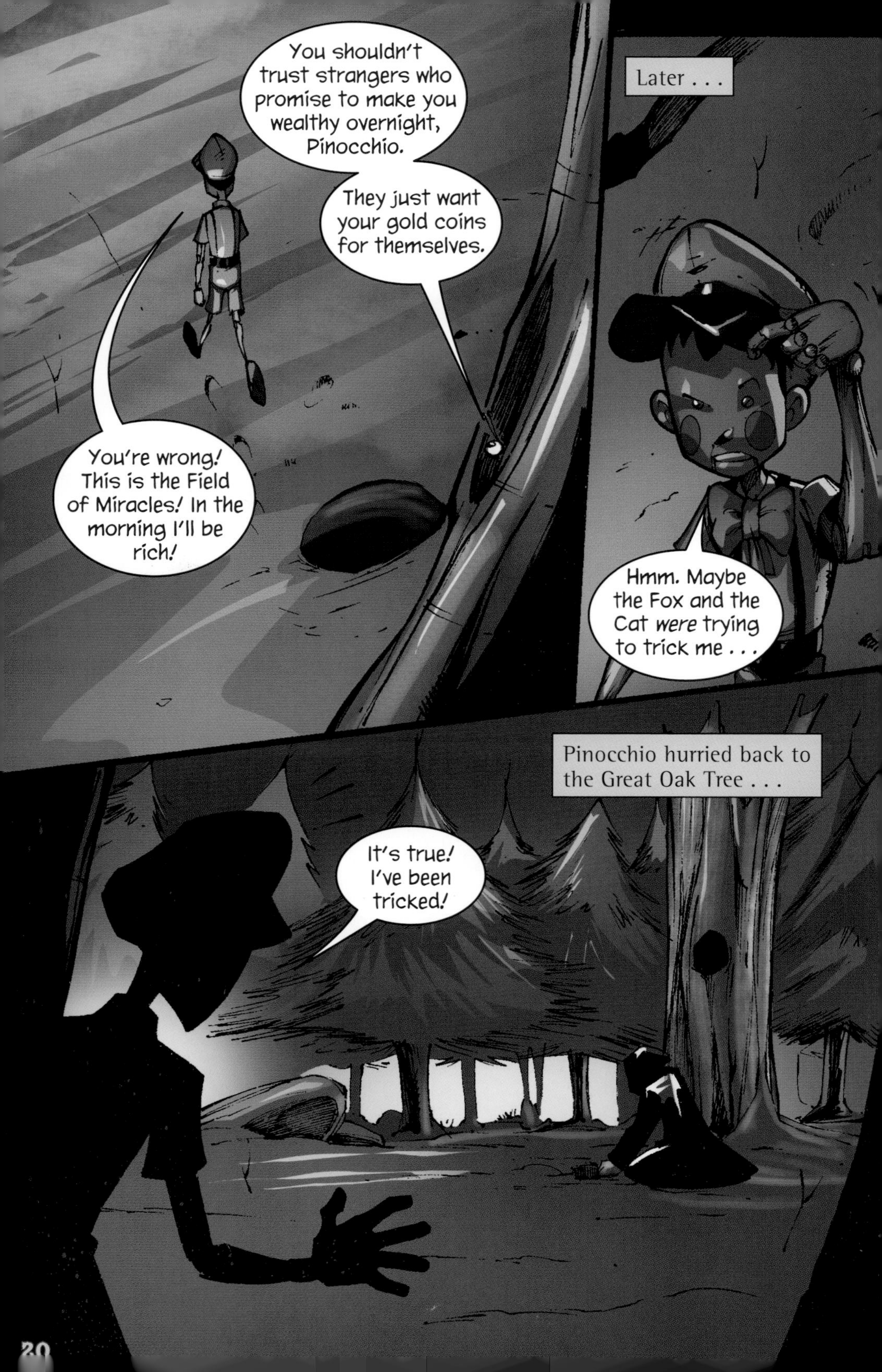
You shouldn't trust strangers who promise to make you wealthy overnight, Pinocchio.
They just want your gold coins for themselves.
You're wrong! This is the Field of Miracles! In the morning I'll be rich!
Later . . .
Hmm. Maybe the Fox and the Cat *were* trying to trick me . . .
Pinocchio hurried back to the Great Oak Tree . . .
It's true! I've been tricked!

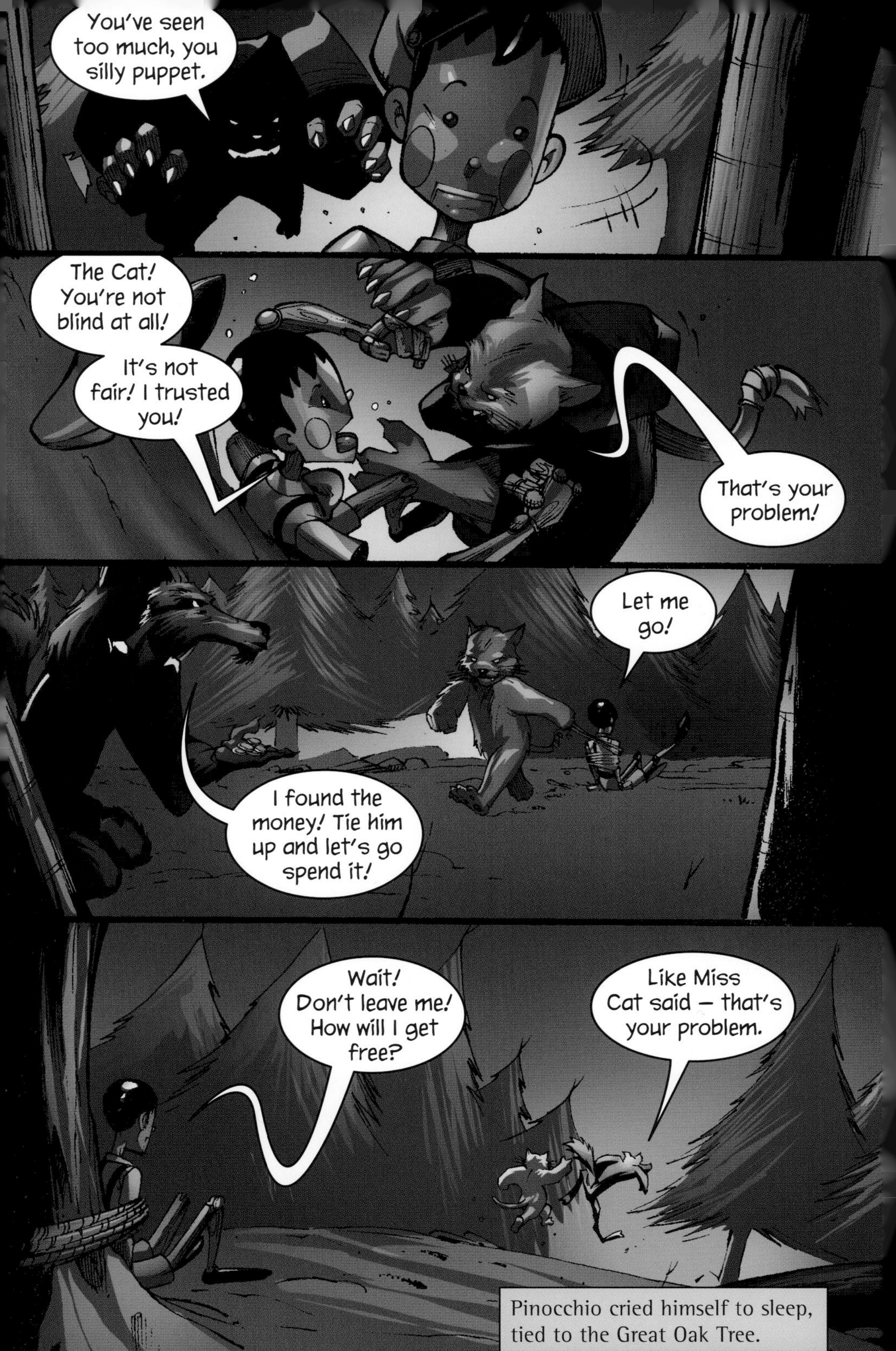
You've seen too much, you silly puppet.
The Cat! You're not blind at all!
It's not fair! I trusted you!
That's your problem!
Let me go!
I found the money! Tie him up and let's go spend it!
Wait! Don't leave me! How will I get free?
Like Miss Cat said — that's your problem.
Pinocchio cried himself to sleep, tied to the Great Oak Tree.

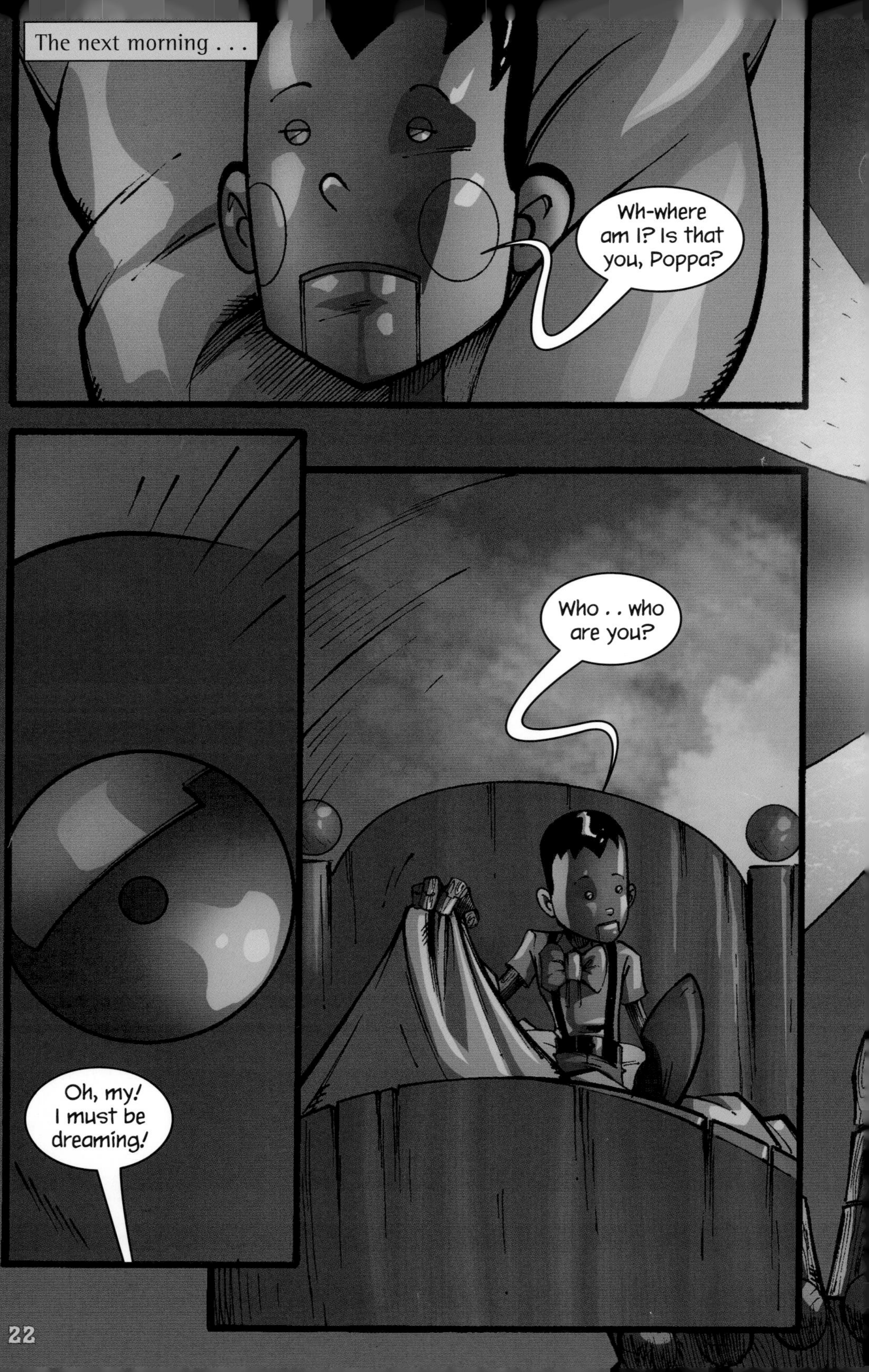
The next morning . . .
Wh-where am I? Is that you, Poppa?
Who . . who are you?
Oh, my! I must be dreaming!

THE BLUE FAIRY

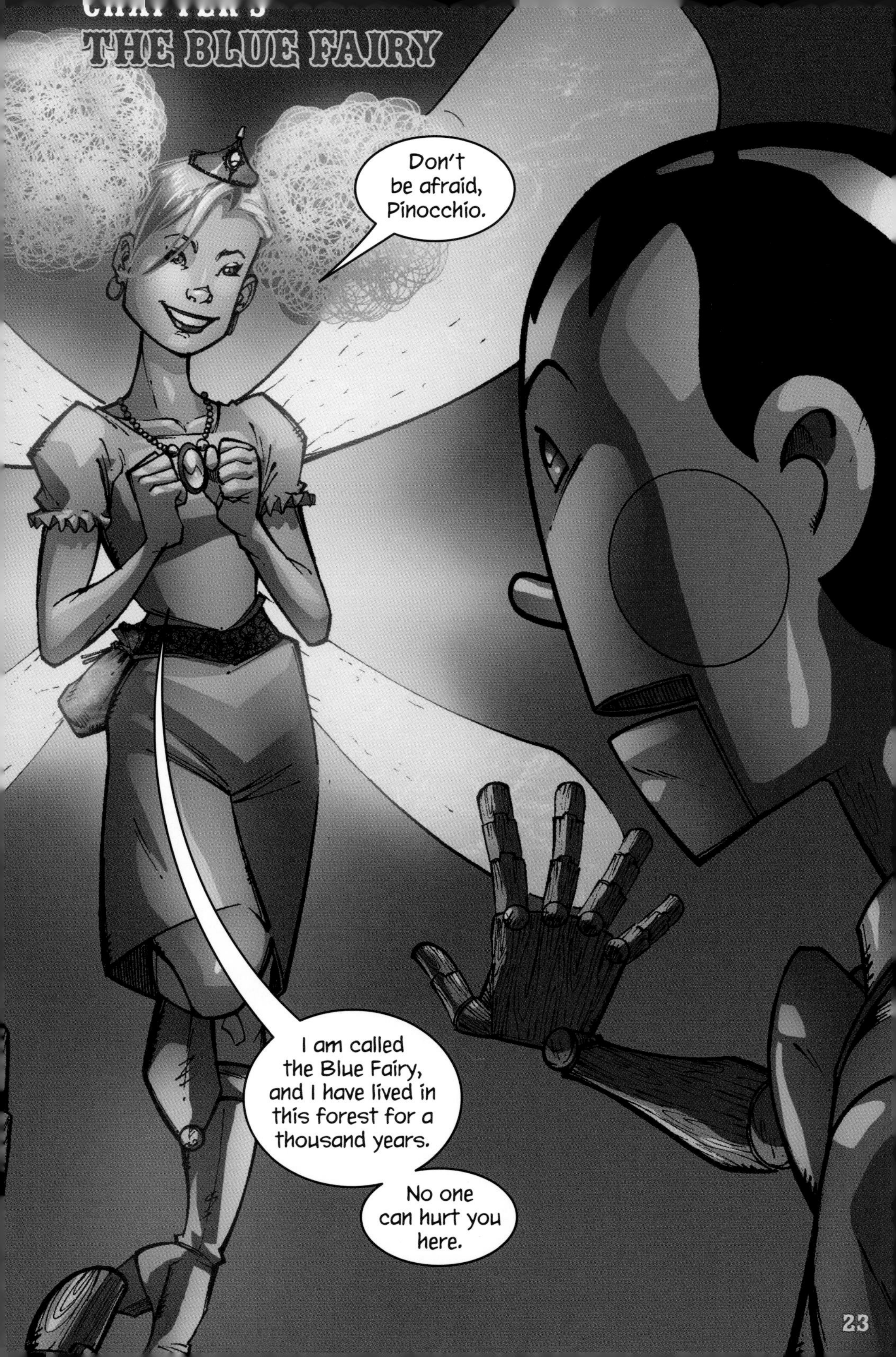
Don't be afraid, Pinocchio.
I am called the Blue Fairy, and I have lived in this forest for a thousand years.
No one can hurt you here.

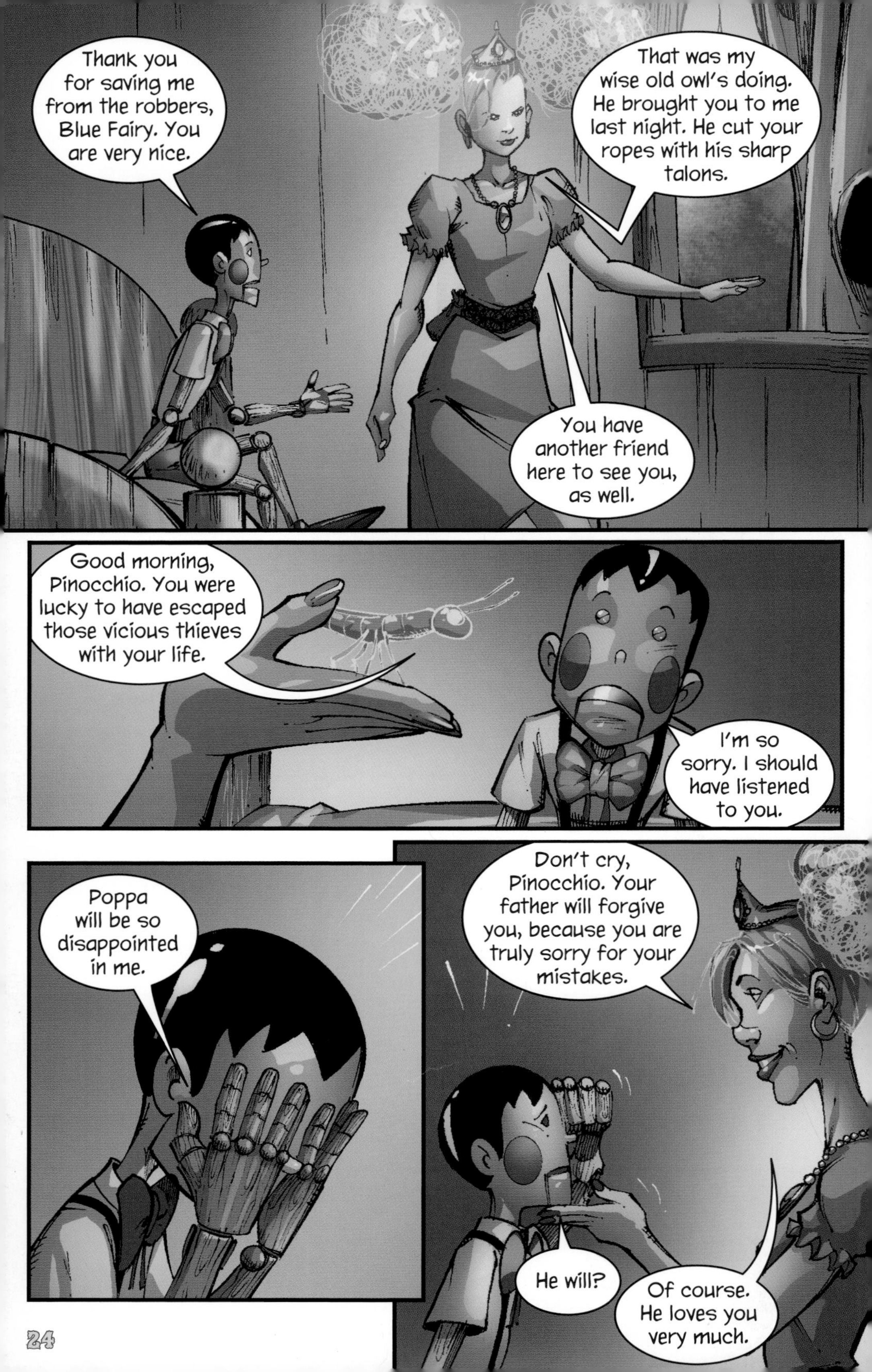
Thank you for saving me from the robbers, Blue Fairy. You are very nice.
That was my wise old owl's doing. He brought you to me last night. He cut your ropes with his sharp talons.
You have another friend here to see you, as well.
Good morning, Pinocchio. You were lucky to have escaped those vicious thieves with your life.
I'm so sorry. I should have listened to you.
Poppa will be so disappointed in me.
Don't cry, Pinocchio. Your father will forgive you, because you are truly sorry for your mistakes.
He will?
Of course. He loves you very much.

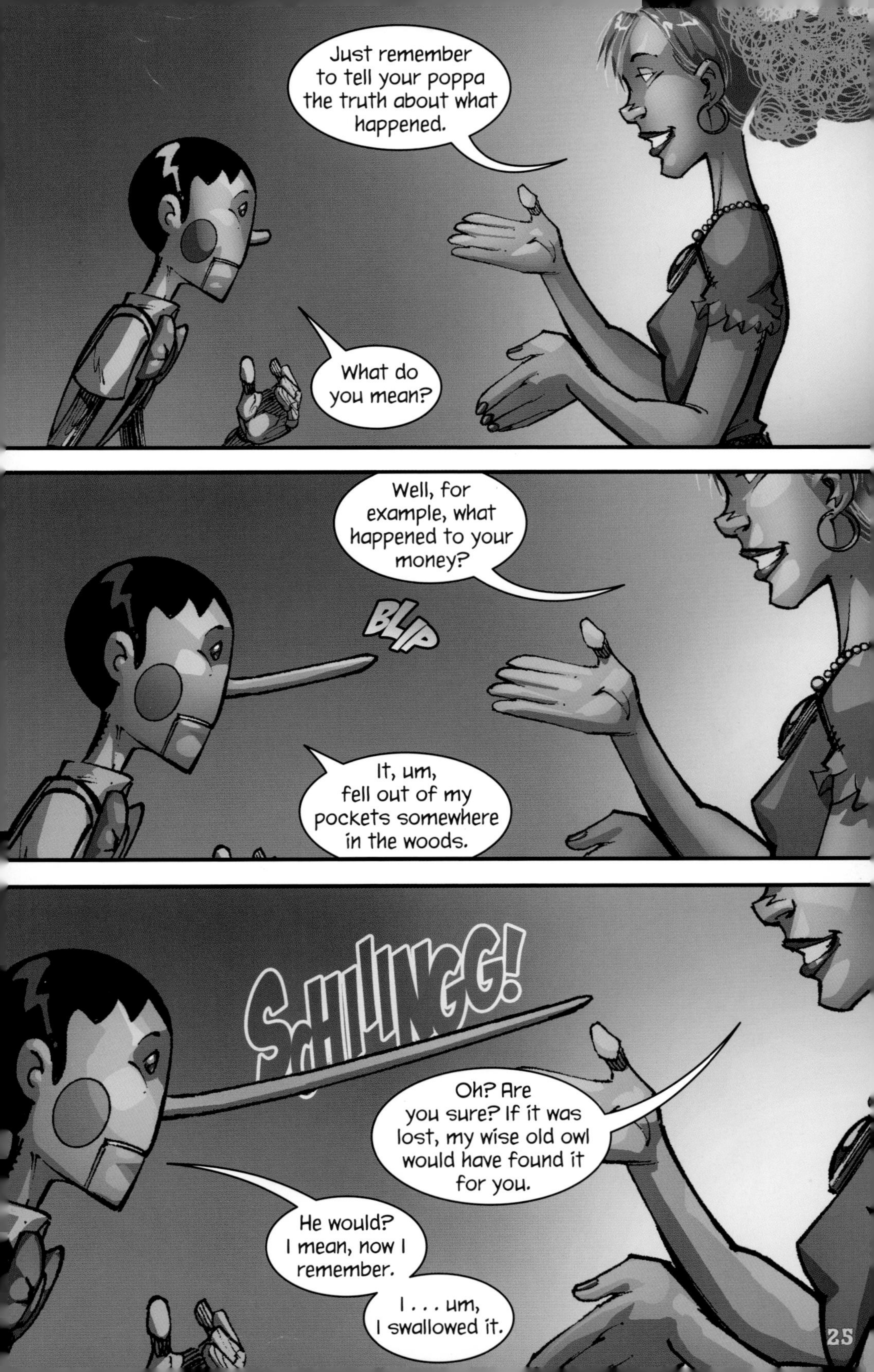

Just remember to tell your poppa the truth about what happened.
What do you mean?
Well, for example, what happened to your money?
BLIP
It, um, fell out of my pockets somewhere in the woods.
SCHLINGG!
Oh? Are you sure? If it was lost, my wise old owl would have found it for you.
He would? I mean, now I remember.
I . . . um, I swallowed it.

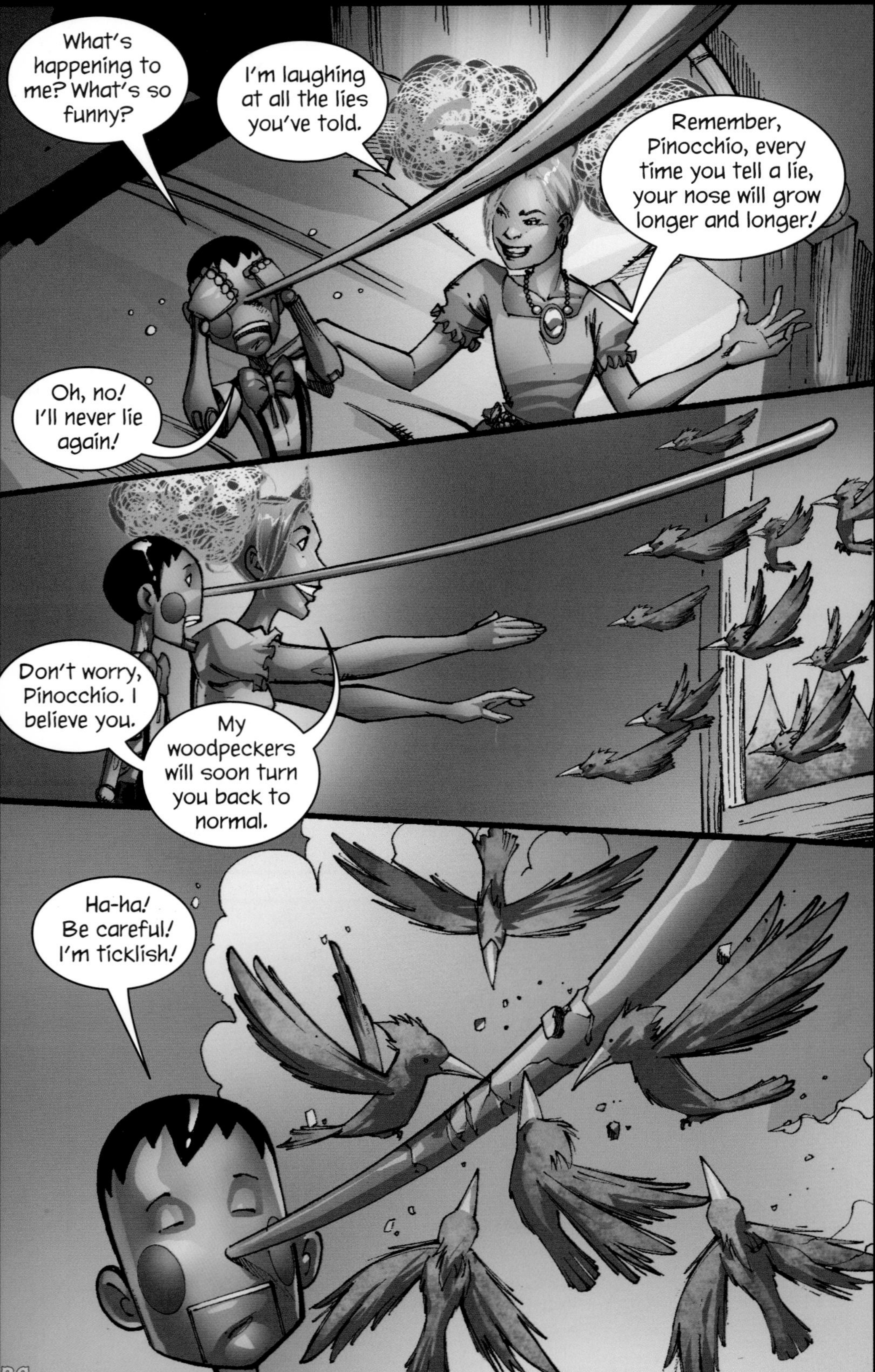
What's happening to me? What's so funny?
I'm laughing at all the lies you've told.
Remember, Pinocchio, every time you tell a lie, your nose will grow longer and longer!
Oh, no! I'll never lie again!
Don't worry, Pinocchio. I believe you.
My woodpeckers will soon turn you back to normal.
Ha-ha! Be careful! I'm ticklish!

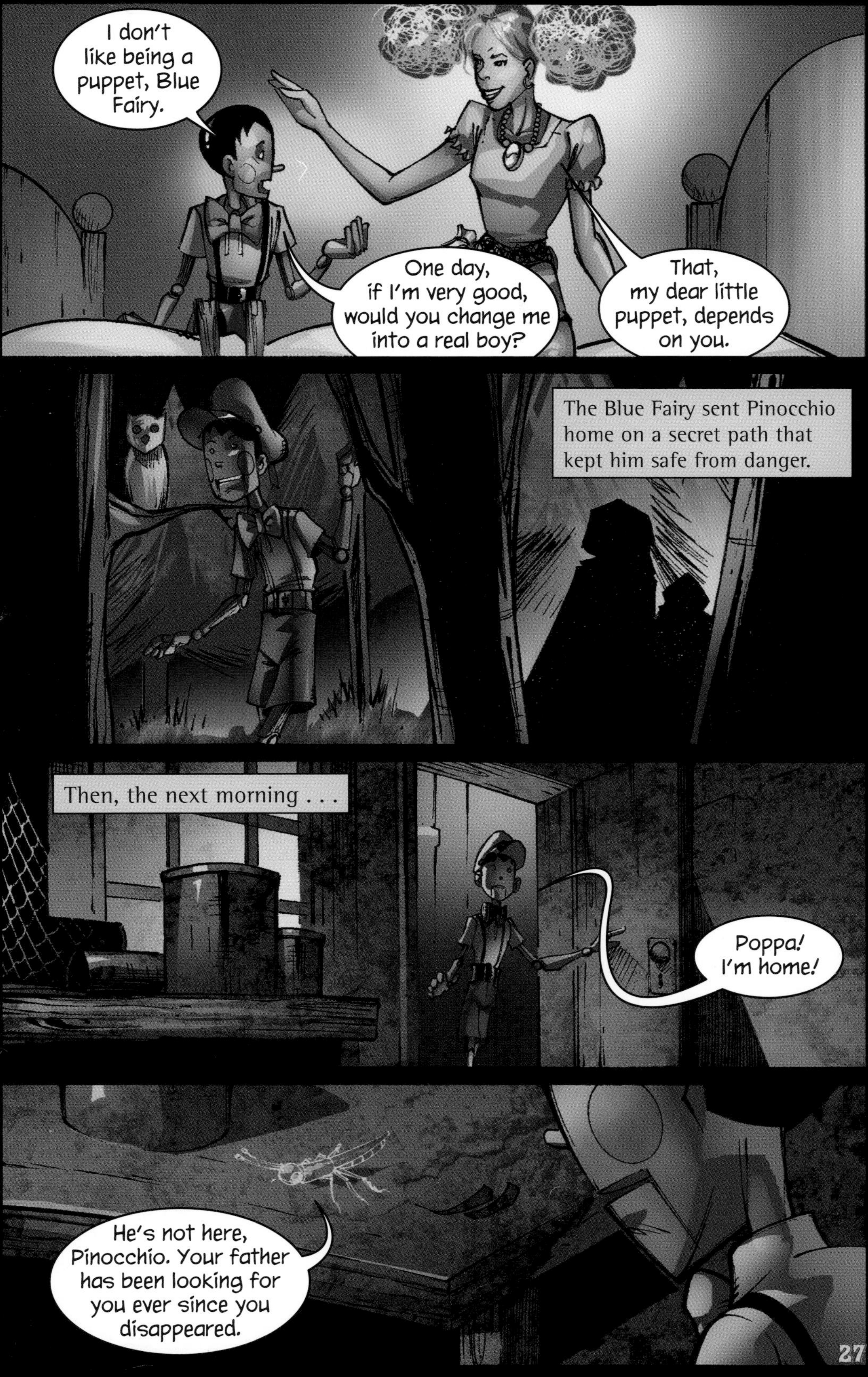

I don't like being a puppet, Blue Fairy.
One day, if I'm very good, would you change me into a real boy?
That, my dear little puppet, depends on you.
The Blue Fairy sent Pinocchio home on a secret path that kept him safe from danger.
Then, the next morning . . .
Poppa! I'm home!
He's not here, Pinocchio. Your father has been looking for you ever since you disappeared.

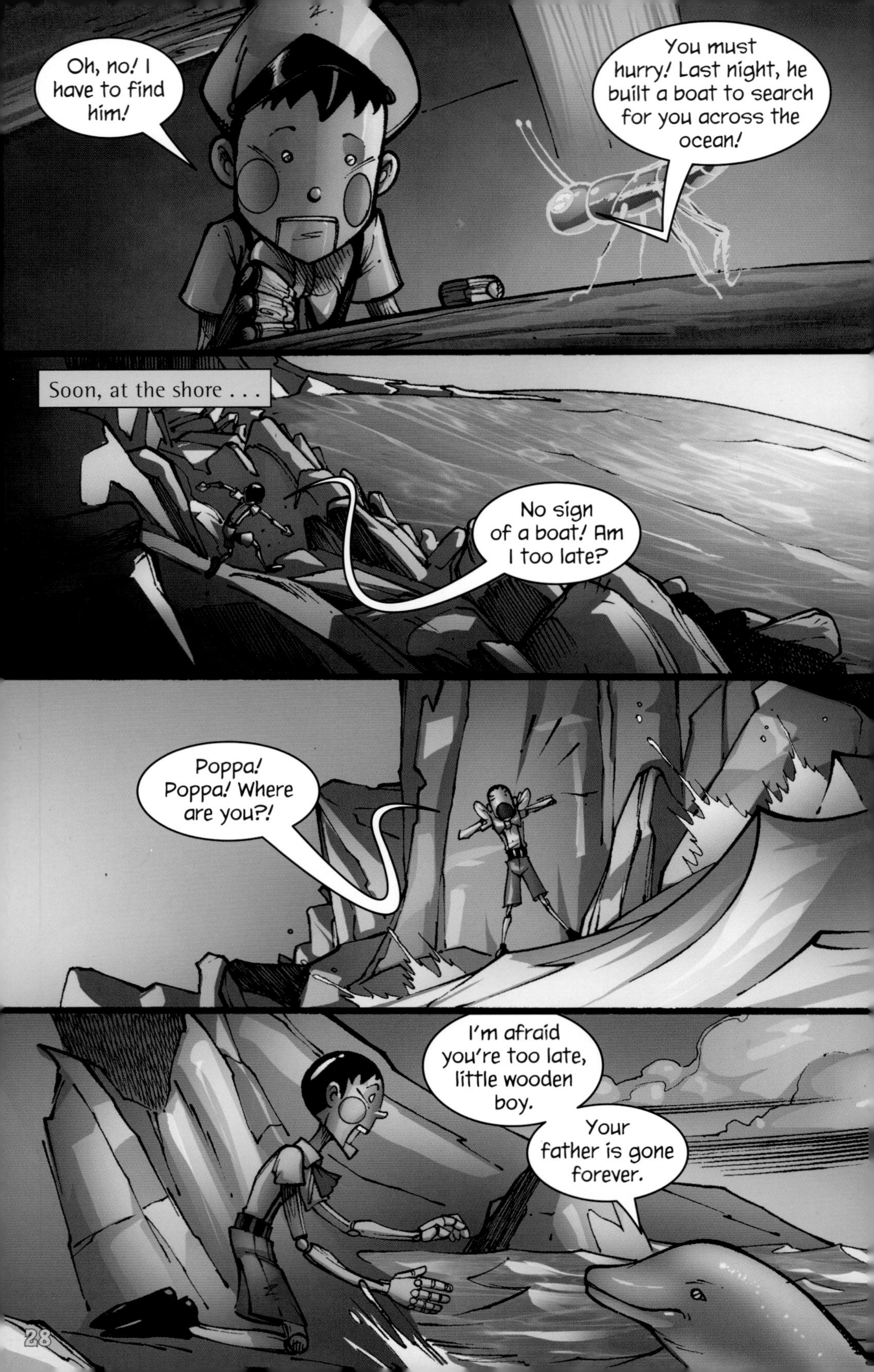
Oh, no! I have to find him!
You must hurry! Last night, he built a boat to search for you across the ocean!
Soon, at the shore . . .
No sign of a boat! Am I too late?
Poppa! Poppa! Where are you?!
I'm afraid you're too late, little wooden boy.
Your father is gone forever.

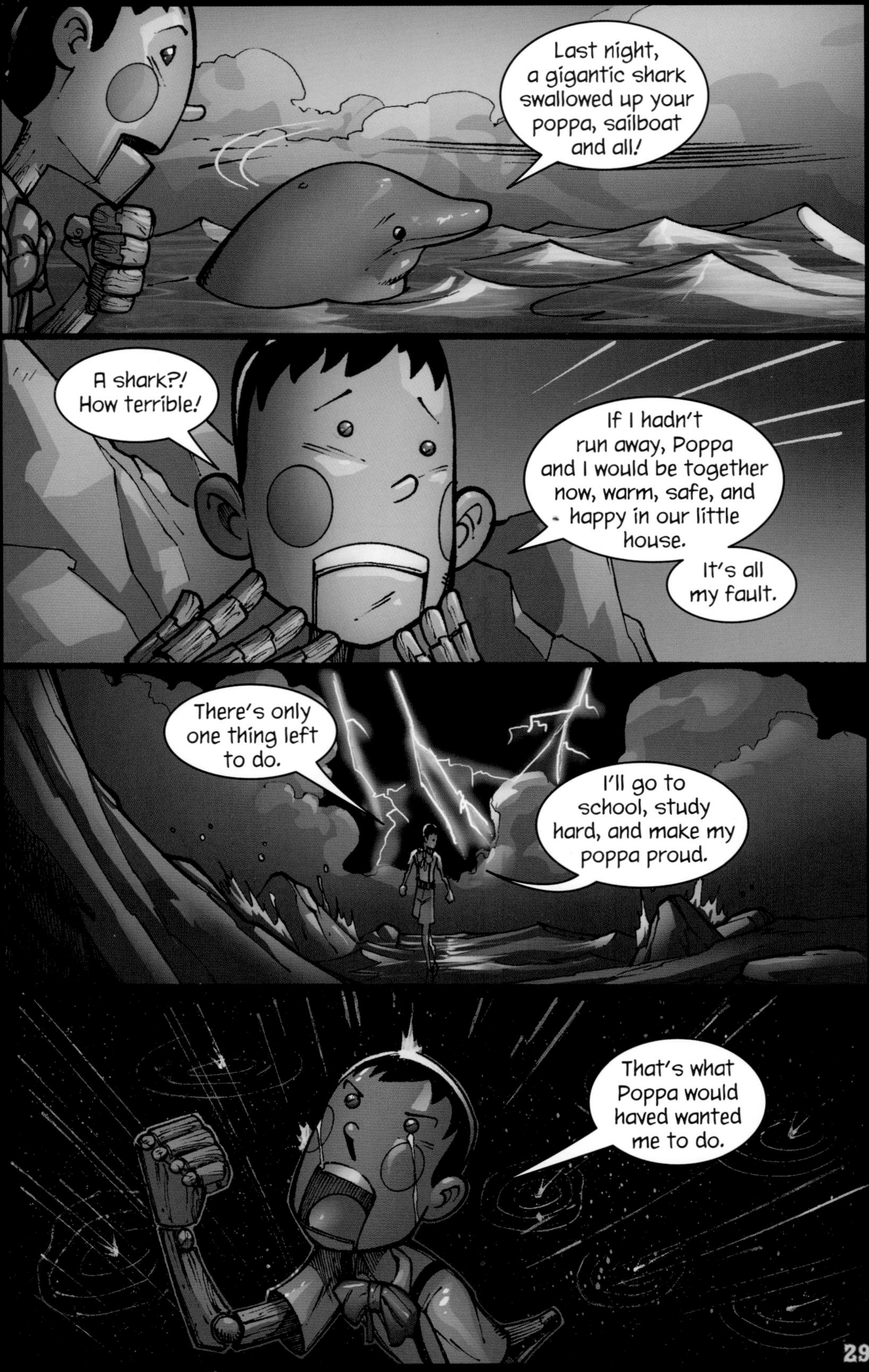

Last night, a gigantic shark swallowed up your poppa, sailboat and all!
A shark?! How terrible!
If I hadn't run away, Poppa and I would be together now, warm, safe, and happy in our little house.
It's all my fault.
There's only one thing left to do.
I'll go to school, study hard, and make my poppa proud.
That's what Poppa would haved wanted me to do.

CHAPTER 4
PLAYLAND

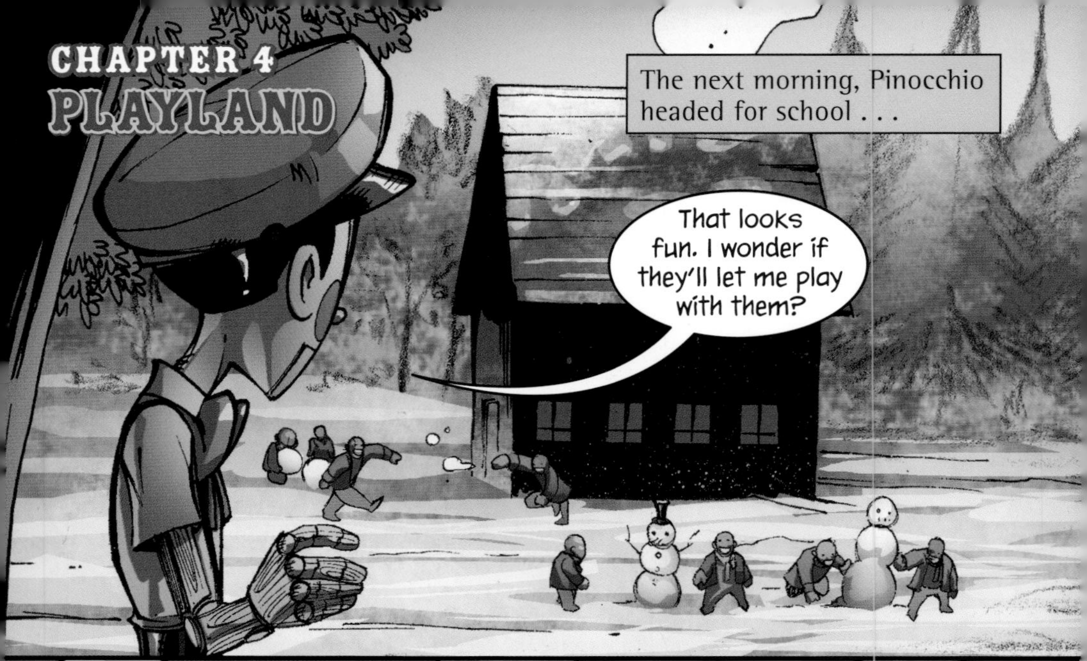
The next morning, Pinocchio headed for school . . .
That looks fun. I wonder if they'll let me play with them?

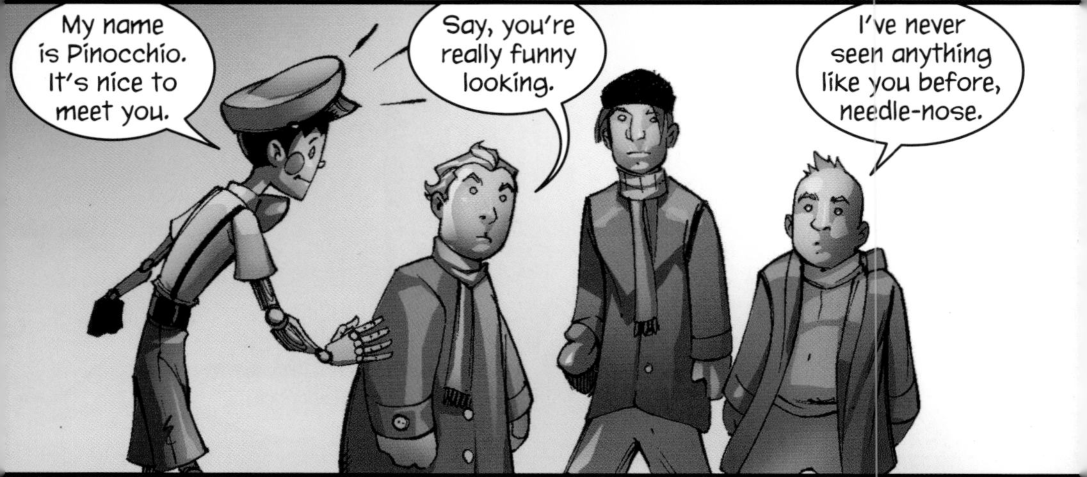
My name is Pinocchio. It's nice to meet you.
Say, you're really funny looking.
I've never seen anything like you before, needle-nose.

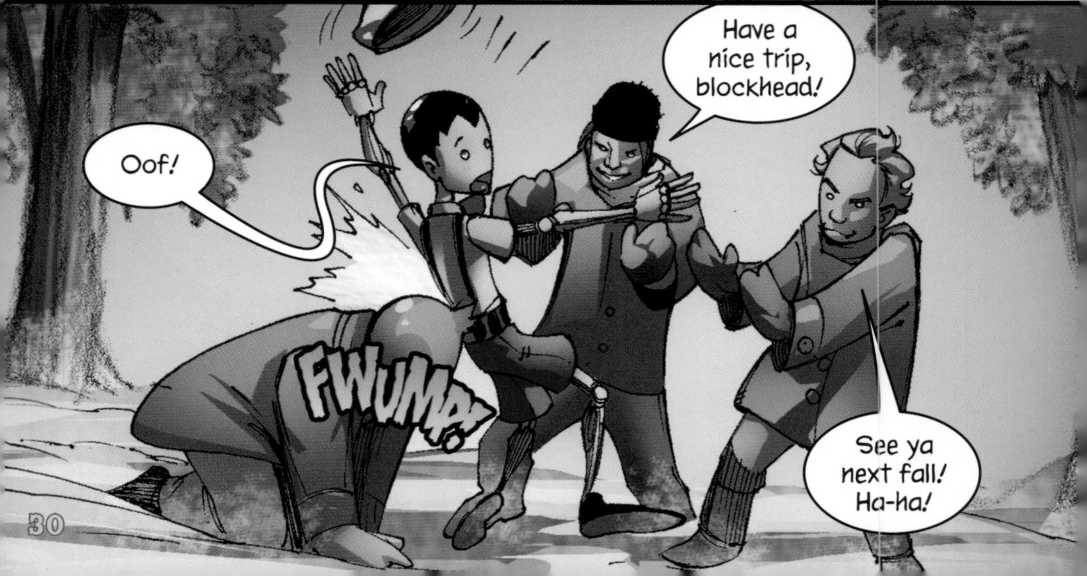
Have a nice trip, blockhead!
Oof!
FWUMP!
See ya next fall! Ha-ha!

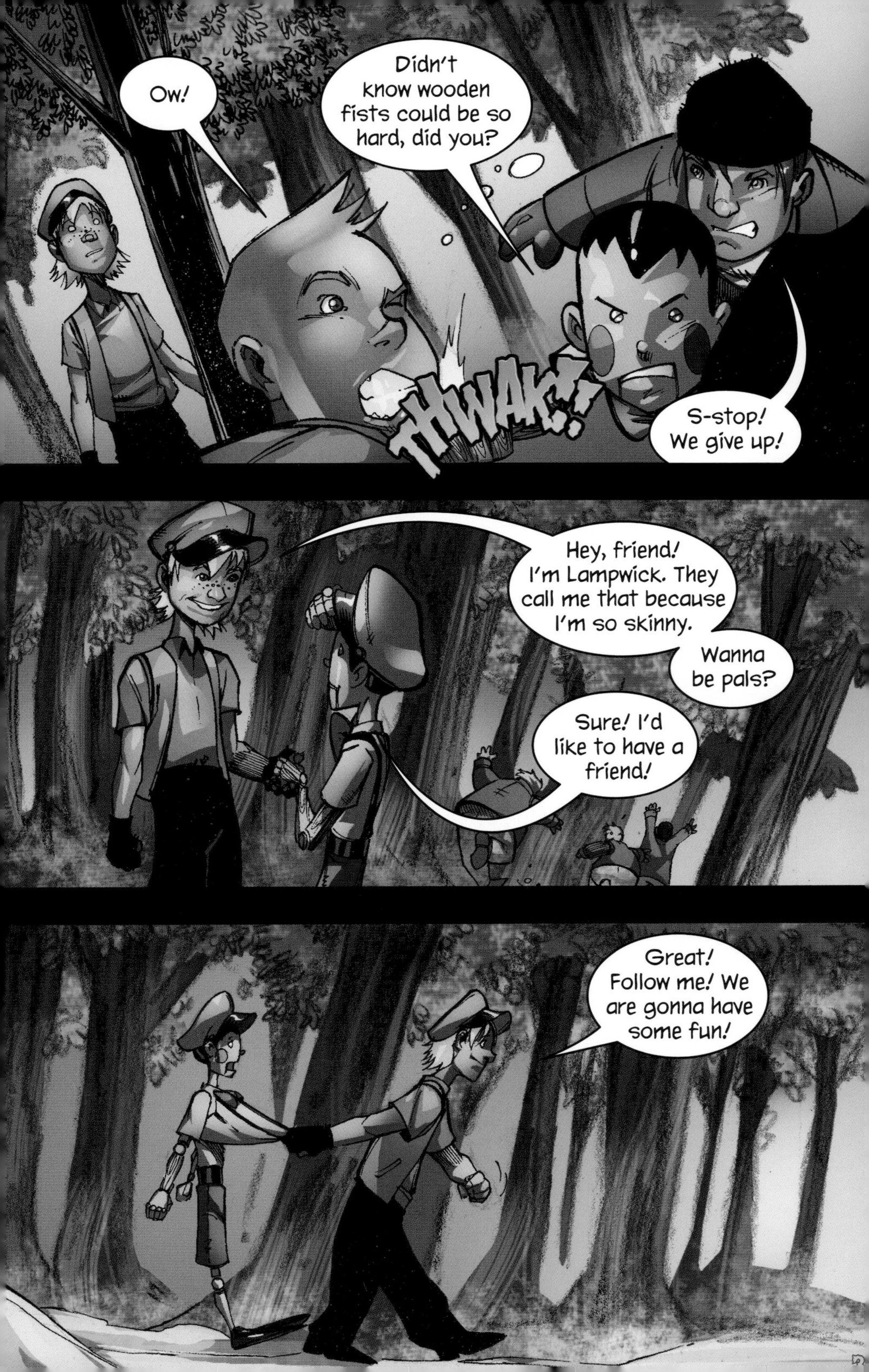
Ow!
Didn't know wooden fists could be so hard, did you?
THWAK!!
S-stop! We give up!
Hey, friend! I'm Lampwick. They call me that because I'm so skinny.
Wanna be pals?
Sure! I'd like to have a friend!
Great! Follow me! We are gonna have some fun!

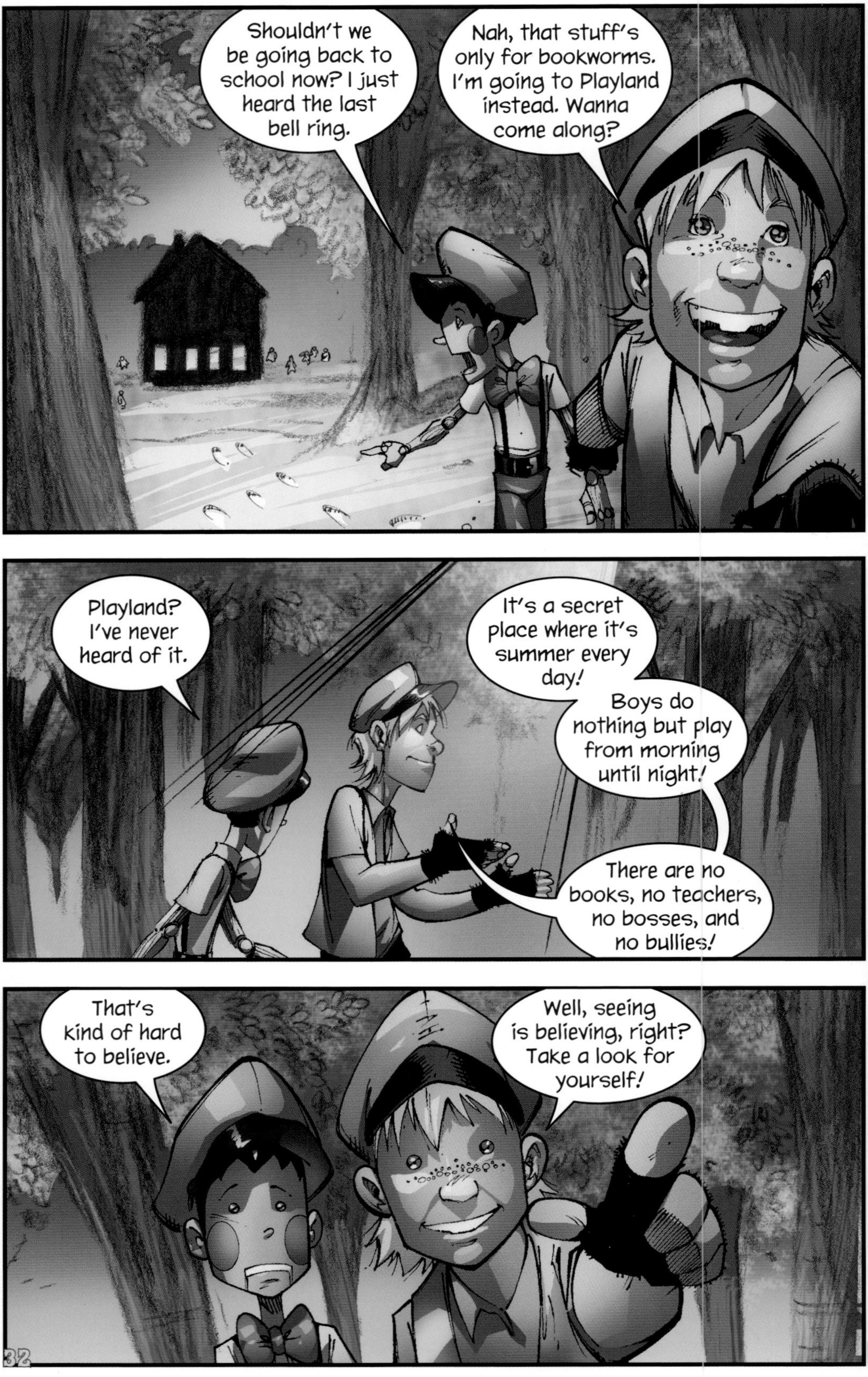
Shouldn't we be going back to school now? I just heard the last bell ring.
Nah, that stuff's only for bookworms. I'm going to Playland instead. Wanna come along?
Playland? I've never heard of it.
It's a secret place where it's summer every day!
Boys do nothing but play from morning until night!
There are no books, no teachers, no bosses, and no bullies!
That's kind of hard to believe.
Well, seeing is believing, right? Take a look for yourself!

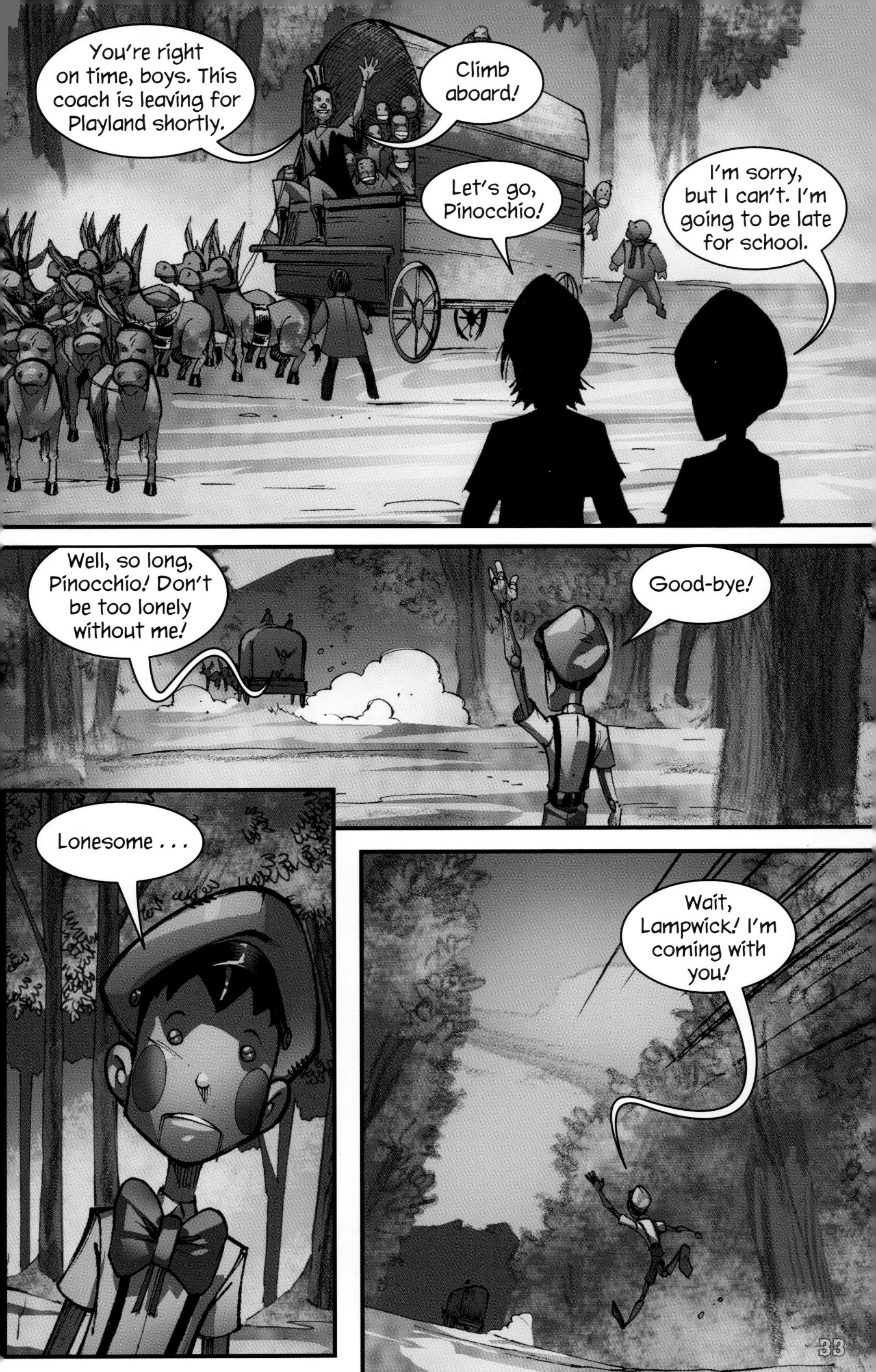
You're right on time, boys. This coach is leaving for Playland shortly.
Climb aboard!
Let's go, Pinocchio!
I'm sorry, but I can't. I'm going to be late for school.
Well, so long, Pinocchio! Don't be too lonely without me!
Good-bye!
Lonesome . . .
Wait, Lampwick! I'm coming with you!

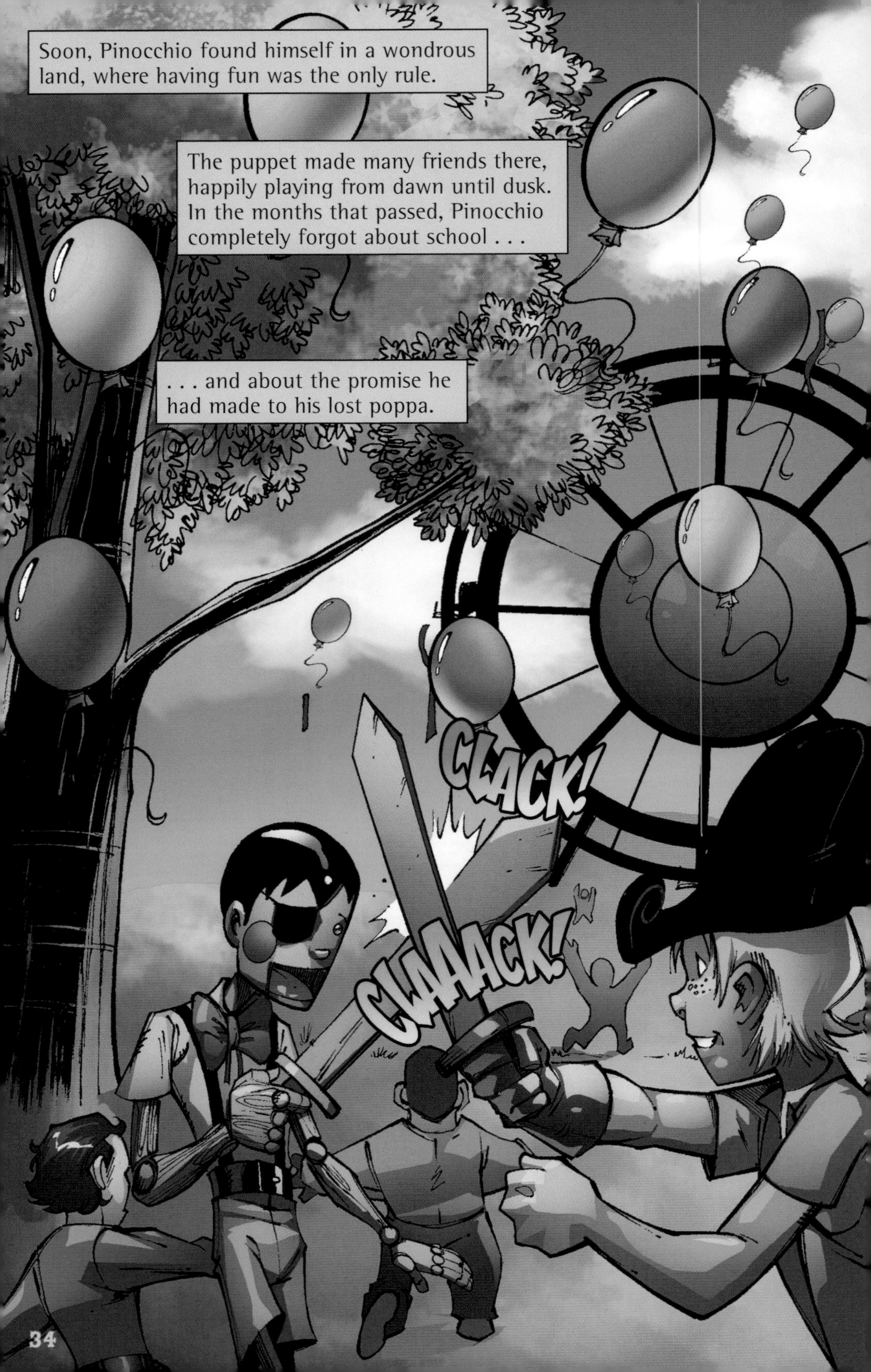
Soon, Pinocchio found himself in a wondrous land, where having fun was the only rule.
The puppet made many friends there, happily playing from dawn until dusk. In the months that passed, Pinocchio completely forgot about school . . .
. . . and about the promise he had made to his lost poppa.
CLACK!
CLAAACK!

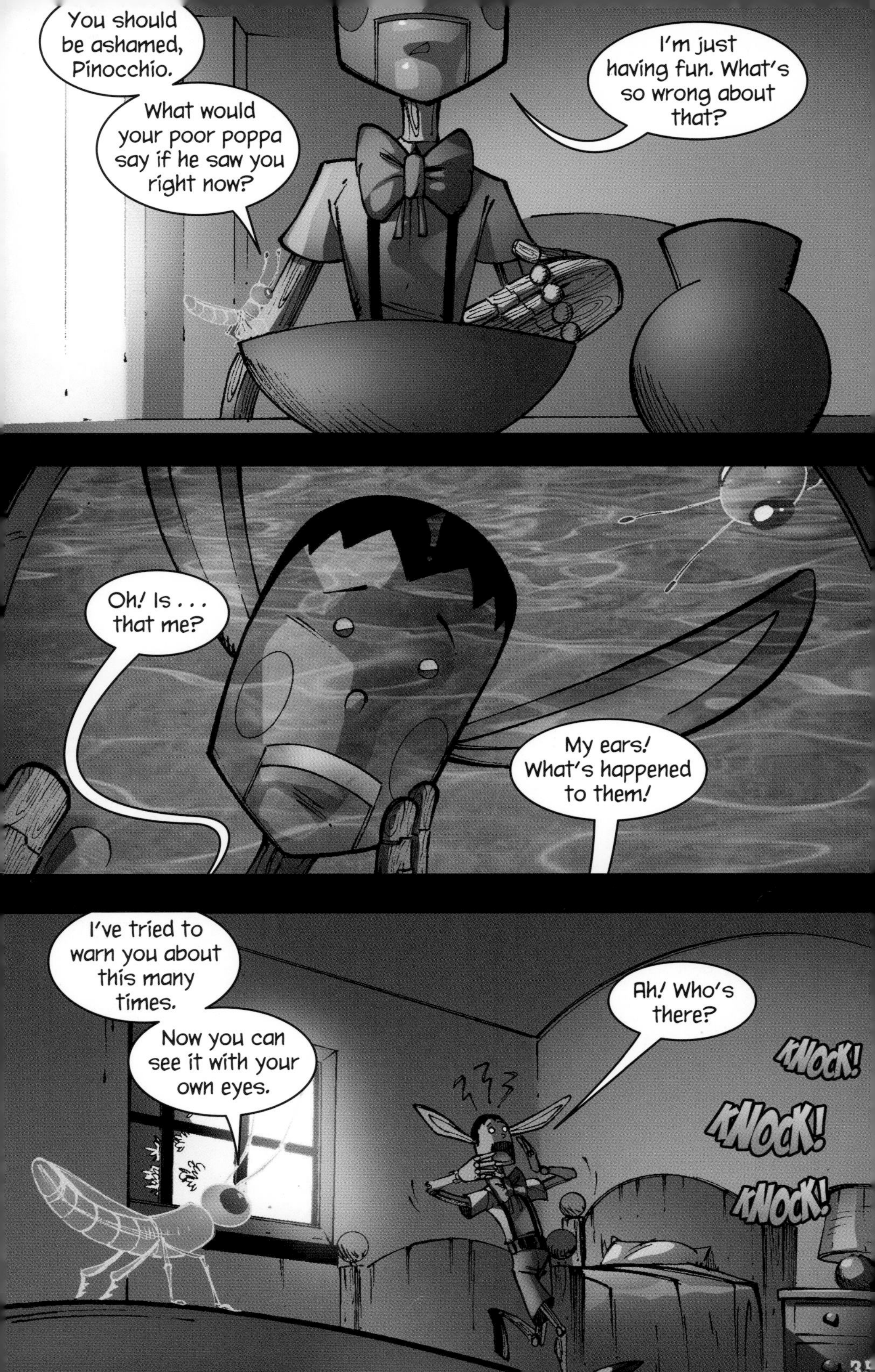

You should be ashamed, Pinocchio.
What would your poor poppa say if he saw you right now?
I'm just having fun. What's so wrong about that?
Oh! Is . . . that me?
My ears! What's happened to them!
I've tried to warn you about this many times.
Now you can see it with your own eyes.
Ah! Who's there?
KNOCK!
KNOCK!
KNOCK!

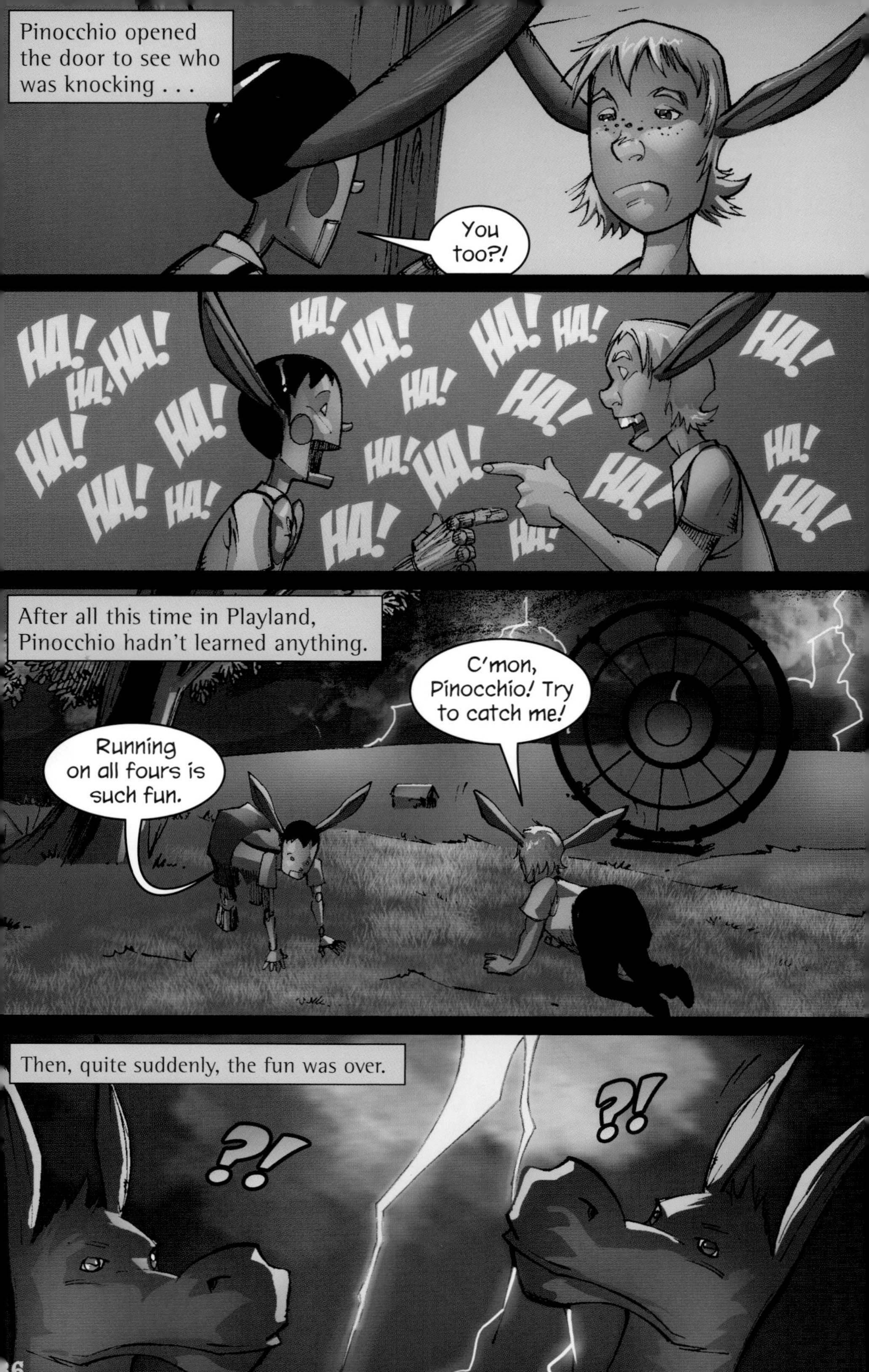
Pinocchio opened the door to see who was knocking . . .
You too?!
HA! HA! HA! HA! HA! HA! HA! HA! HA! HA! HA! HA! HA! HA! HA! HA! HA! HA! HA! HA! HA!
After all this time in Playland, Pinocchio hadn't learned anything.
C'mon, Pinocchio! Try to catch me!
Running on all fours is such fun.
Then, quite suddenly, the fun was over.
?!
?!

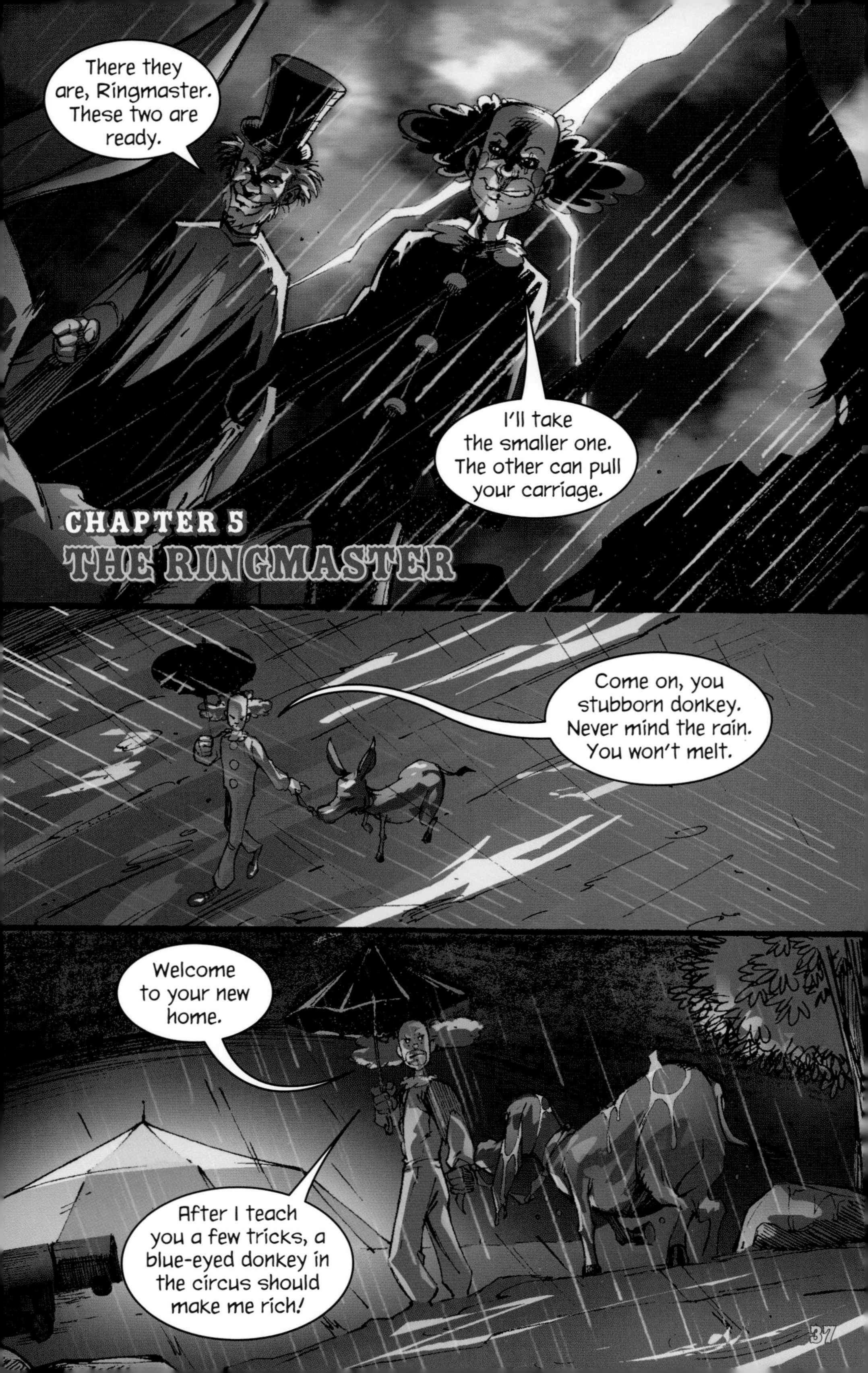
There they are, Ringmaster. These two are ready.
I'll take the smaller one. The other can pull your carriage.
CHAPTER 5
THE RINGMASTER
Come on, you stubborn donkey. Never mind the rain. You won't melt.
Welcome to your new home.
After I teach you a few tricks, a blue-eyed donkey in the circus should make me rich!

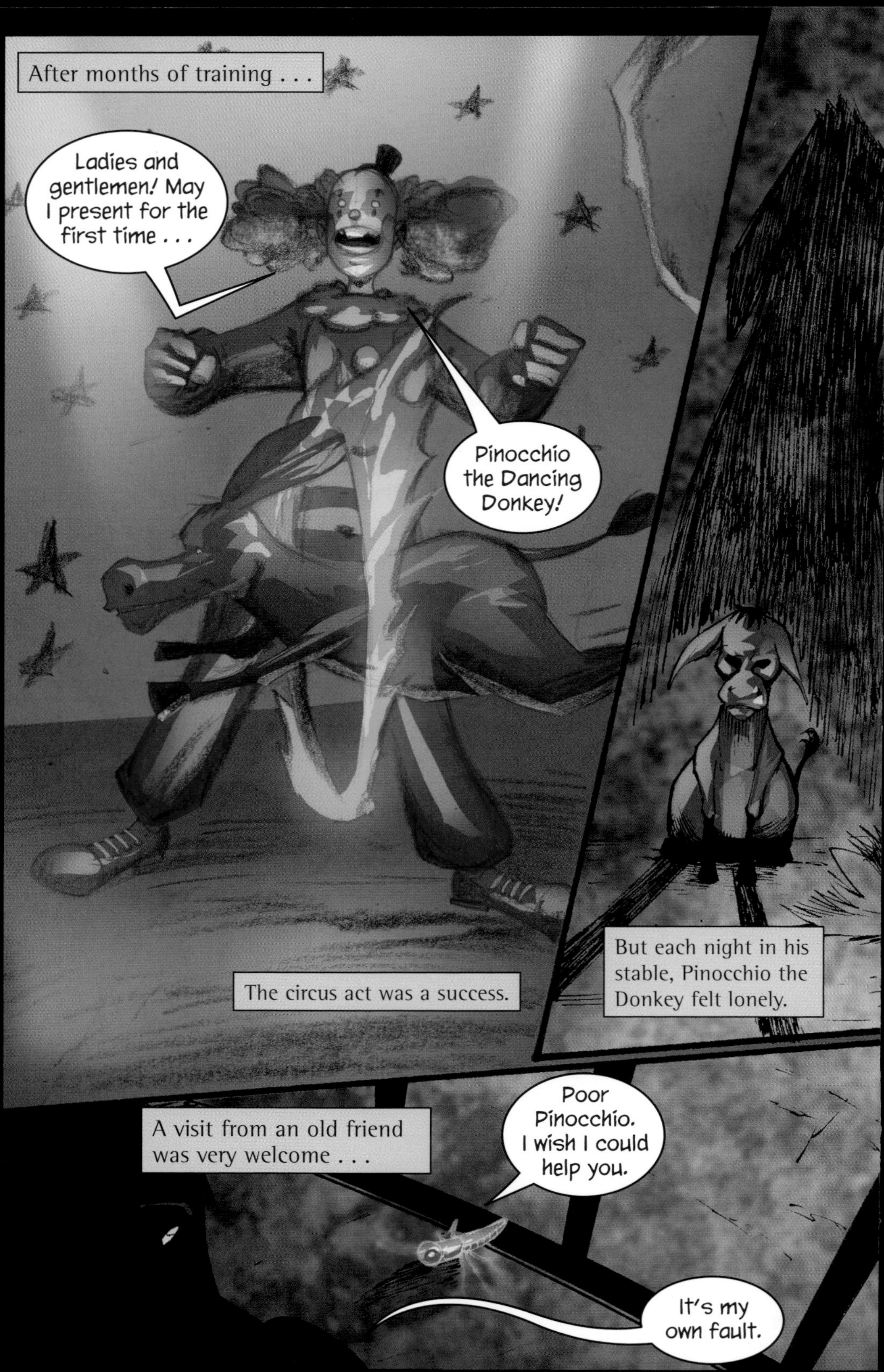
After months of training . . .
Ladies and gentlemen! May I present for the first time . . .
Pinocchio the Dancing Donkey!
The circus act was a success.
But each night in his stable, Pinocchio the Donkey felt lonely.
A visit from an old friend was very welcome . . .
Poor Pinocchio. I wish I could help you.
It's my own fault.

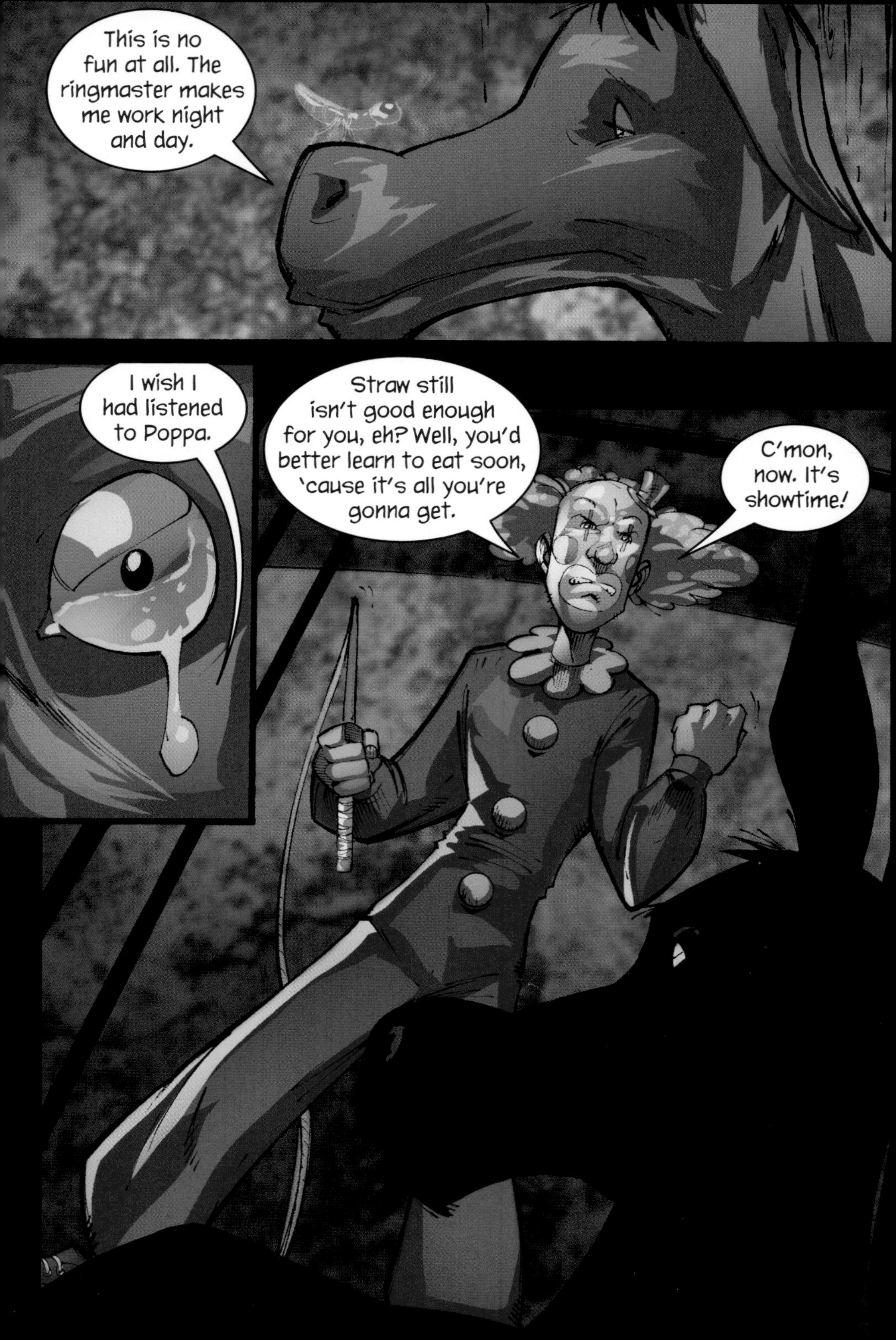
This is no fun at all. The ringmaster makes me work night and day.
I wish I had listened to Poppa.
Straw still isn't good enough for you, eh? Well, you'd better learn to eat soon, 'cause it's all you're gonna get.
C'mon, now. It's showtime!

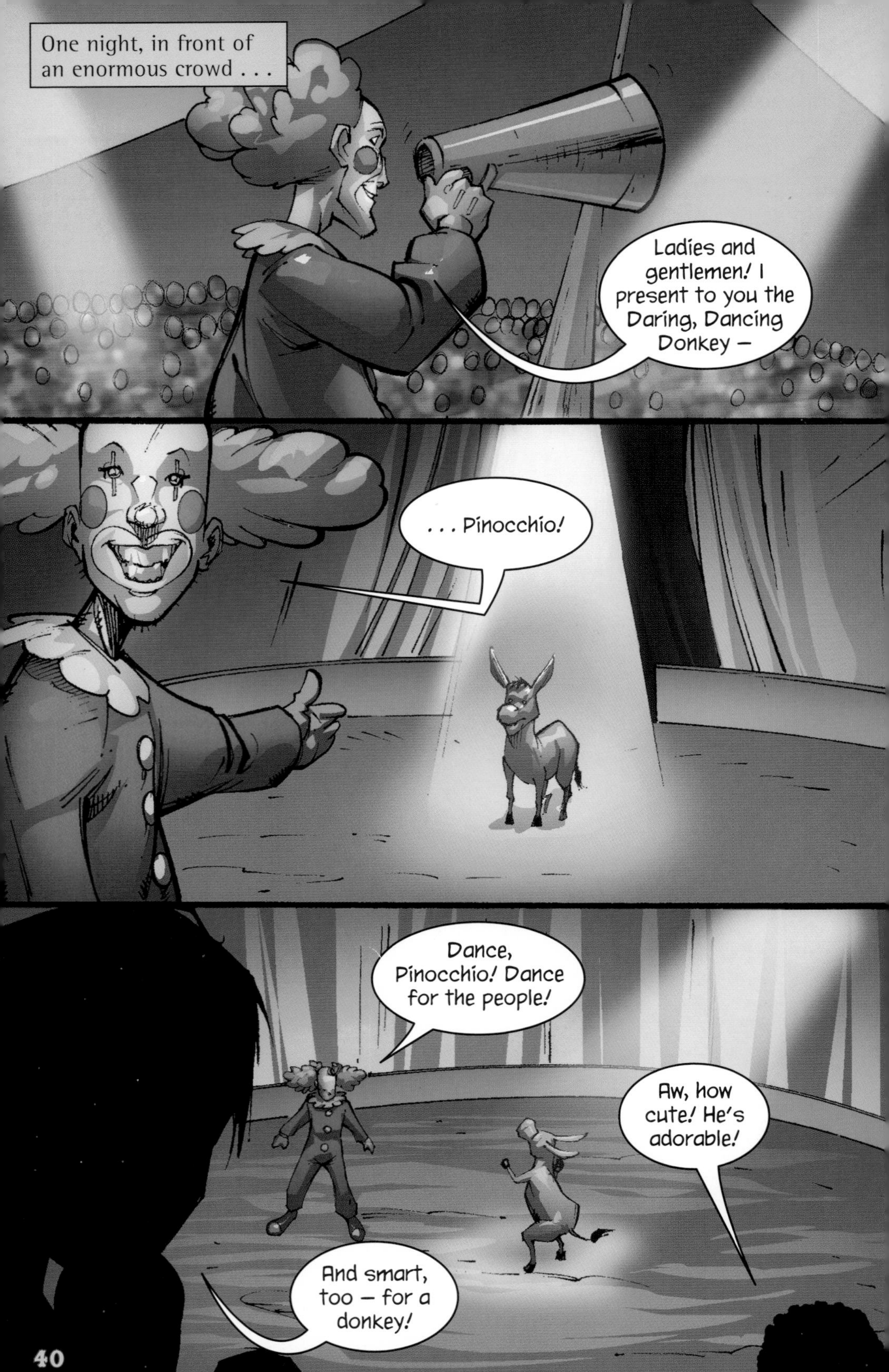
One night, in front of an enormous crowd . . .
Ladies and gentlemen! I present to you the Daring, Dancing Donkey —
. . . Pinocchio!
Dance, Pinocchio! Dance for the people!
Aw, how cute! He's adorable!
And smart, too — for a donkey!

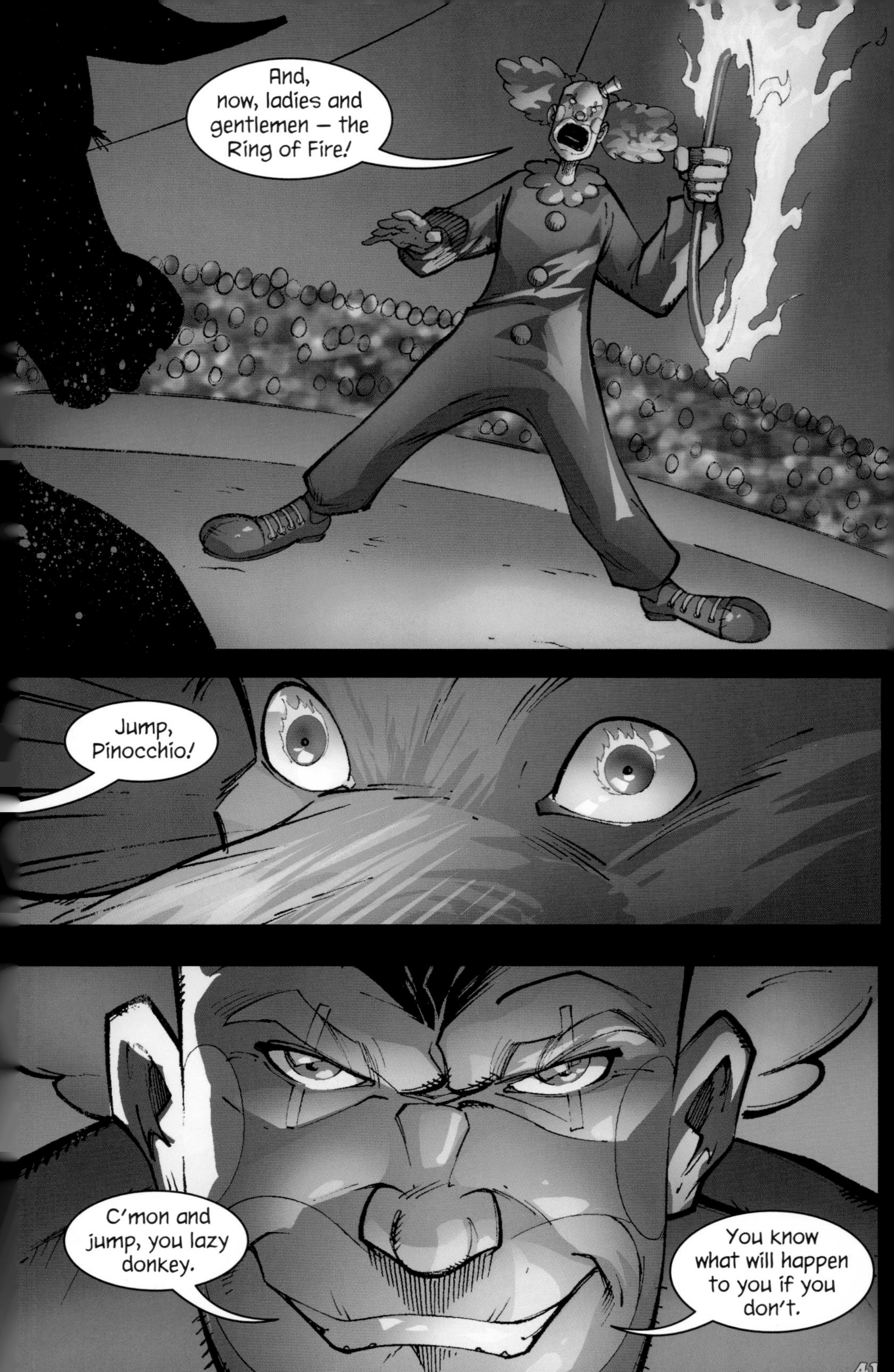
And, now, ladies and gentlemen — the Ring of Fire!
Jump, Pinocchio!
C'mon and jump, you lazy donkey.
You know what will happen to you if you don't.

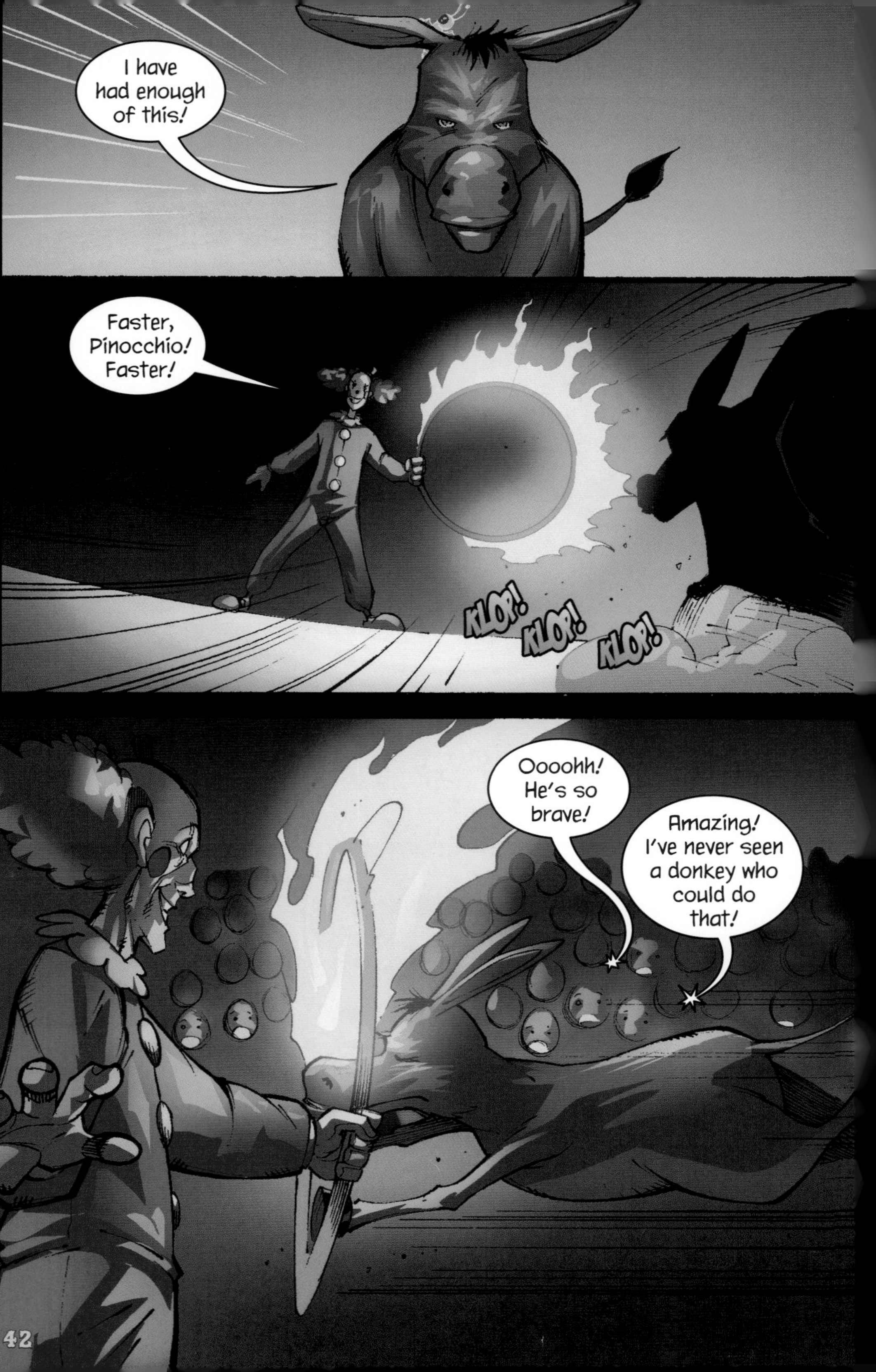

I have had enough of this!
Faster, Pinocchio! Faster!
KLOP! KLOP! KLOP!
Oooohh! He's so brave!
Amazing! I've never seen a donkey who could do that!

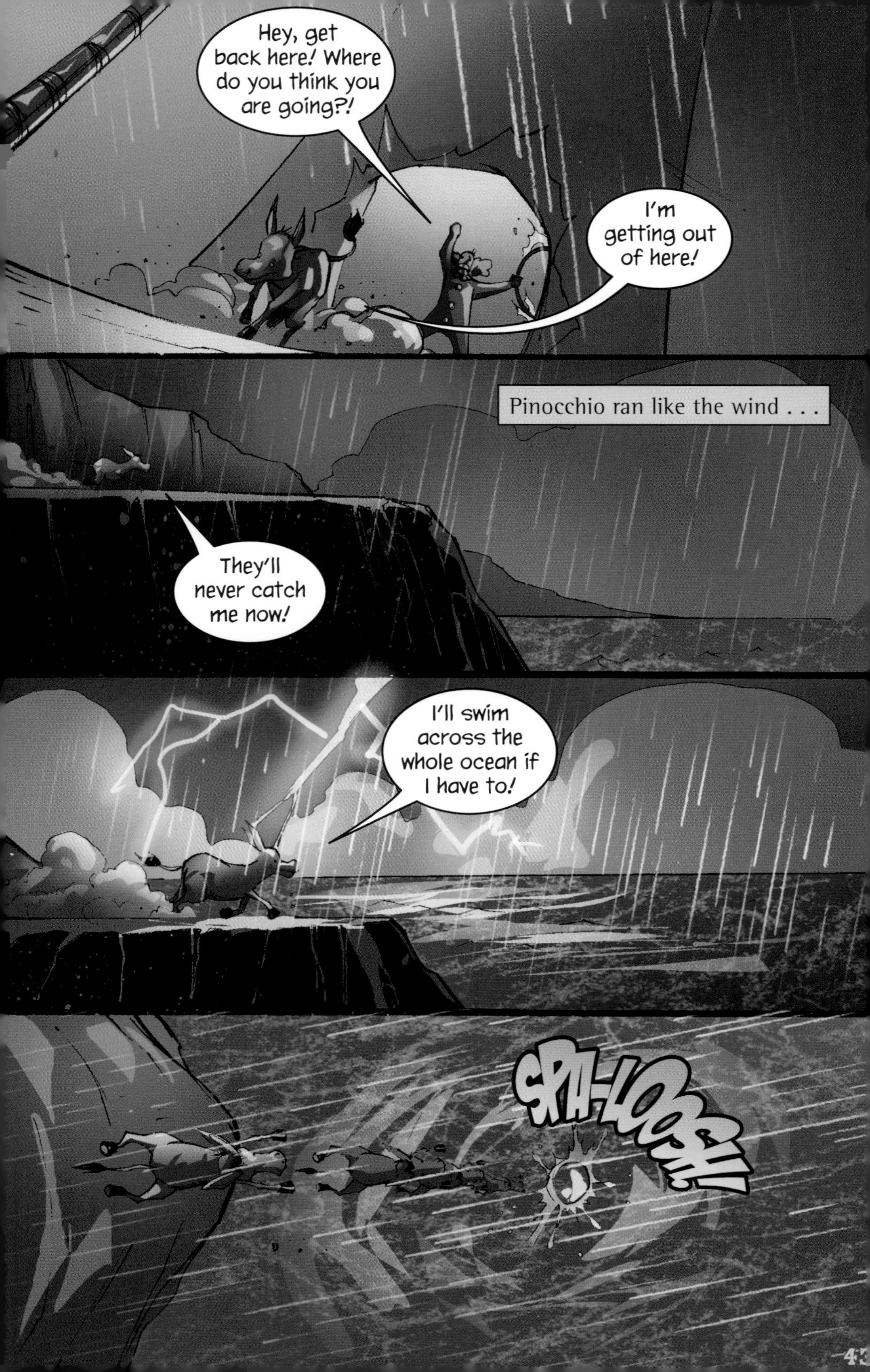
Hey, get back here! Where do you think you are going?!
I'm getting out of here!
Pinocchio ran like the wind . . .
They'll never catch me now!
I'll swim across the whole ocean if I have to!
SPLA-LOOSH!!

CHAPTER 6
LOST AT SEA

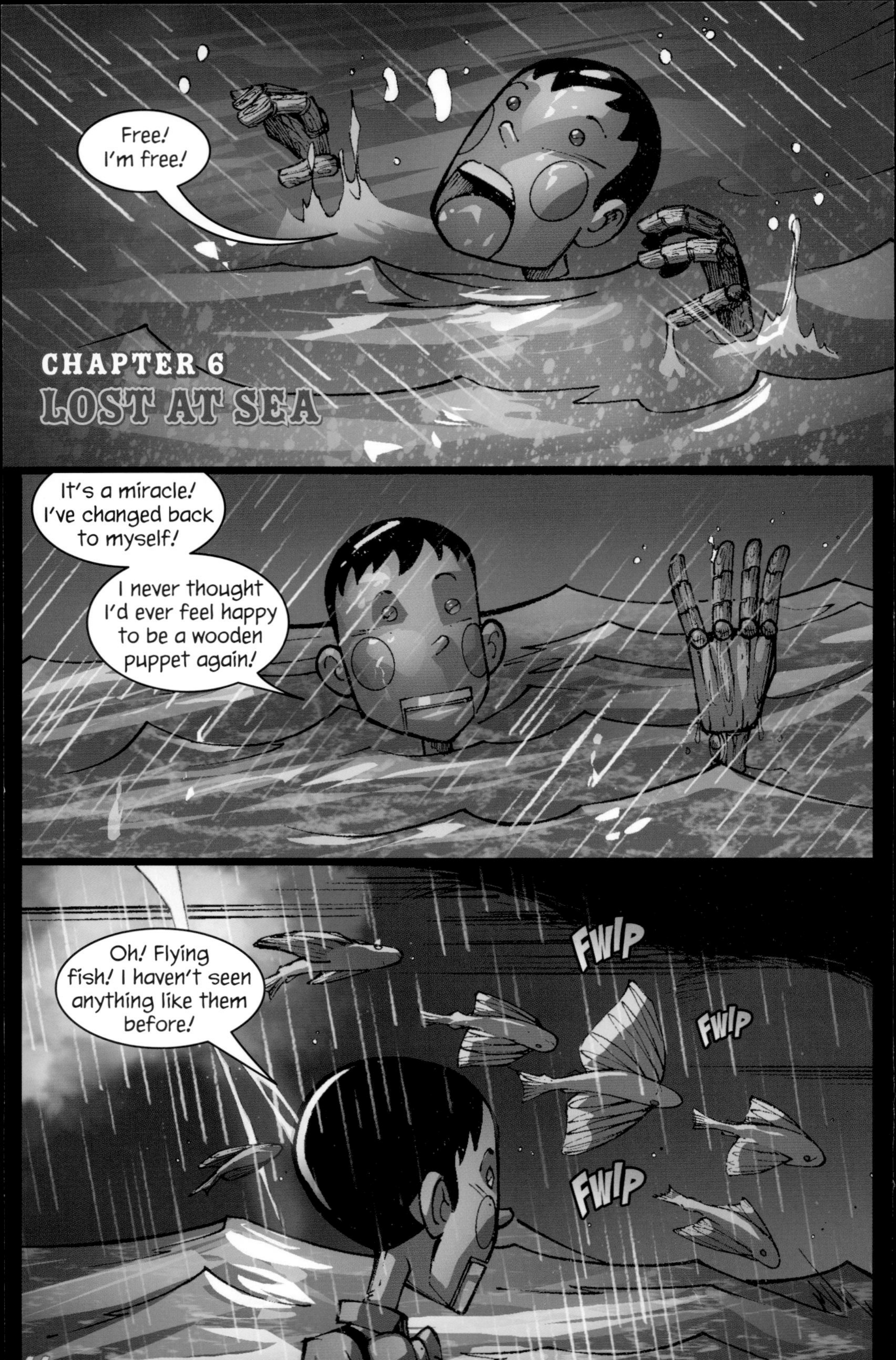
Free! I'm free!
It's a miracle! I've changed back to myself!
I never thought I'd ever feel happy to be a wooden puppet again!
Oh! Flying fish! I haven't seen anything like them before!
FWIP
FWIP
FWIP

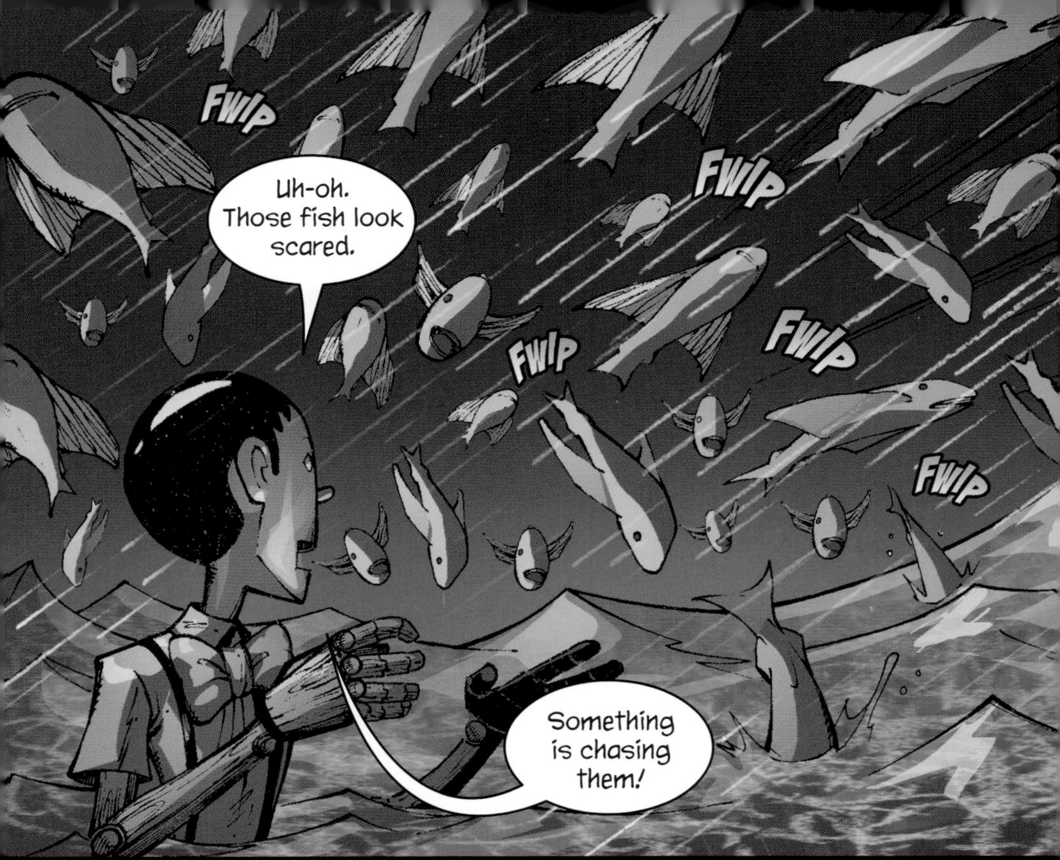
FWIP
Uh-oh. Those fish look scared.
FWIP
FWIP
FWIP
FWIP
Something is chasing them!

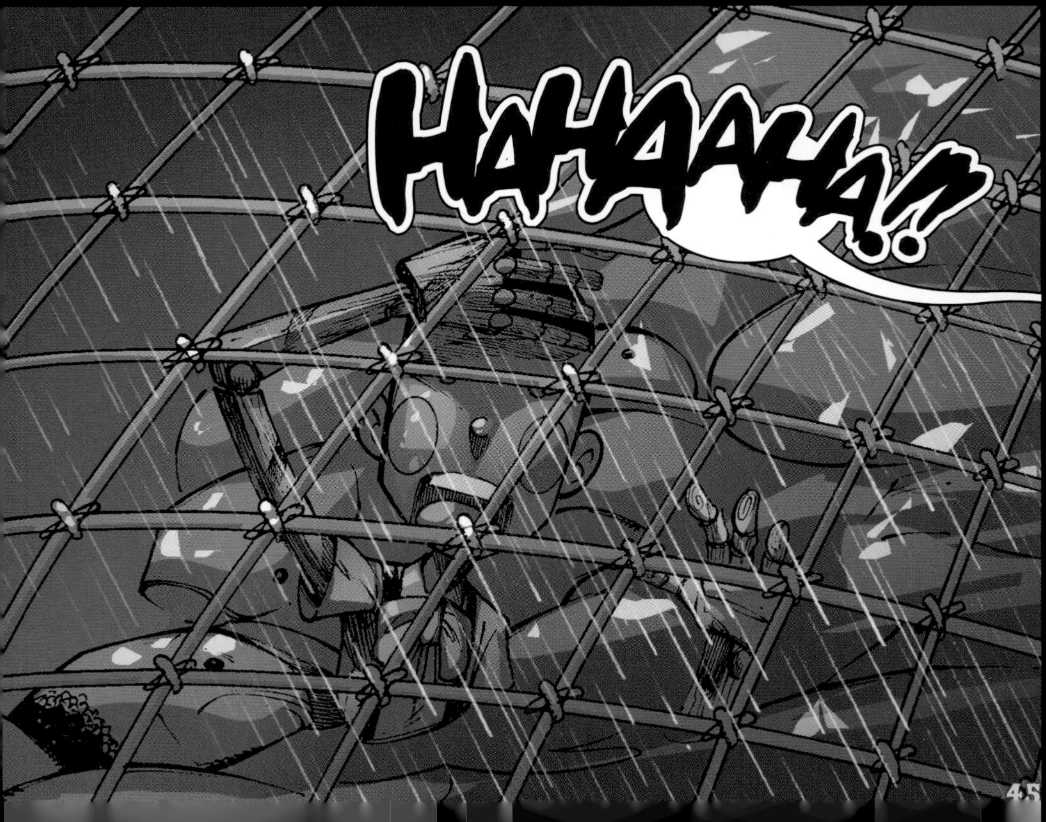
HAHAAHA!!

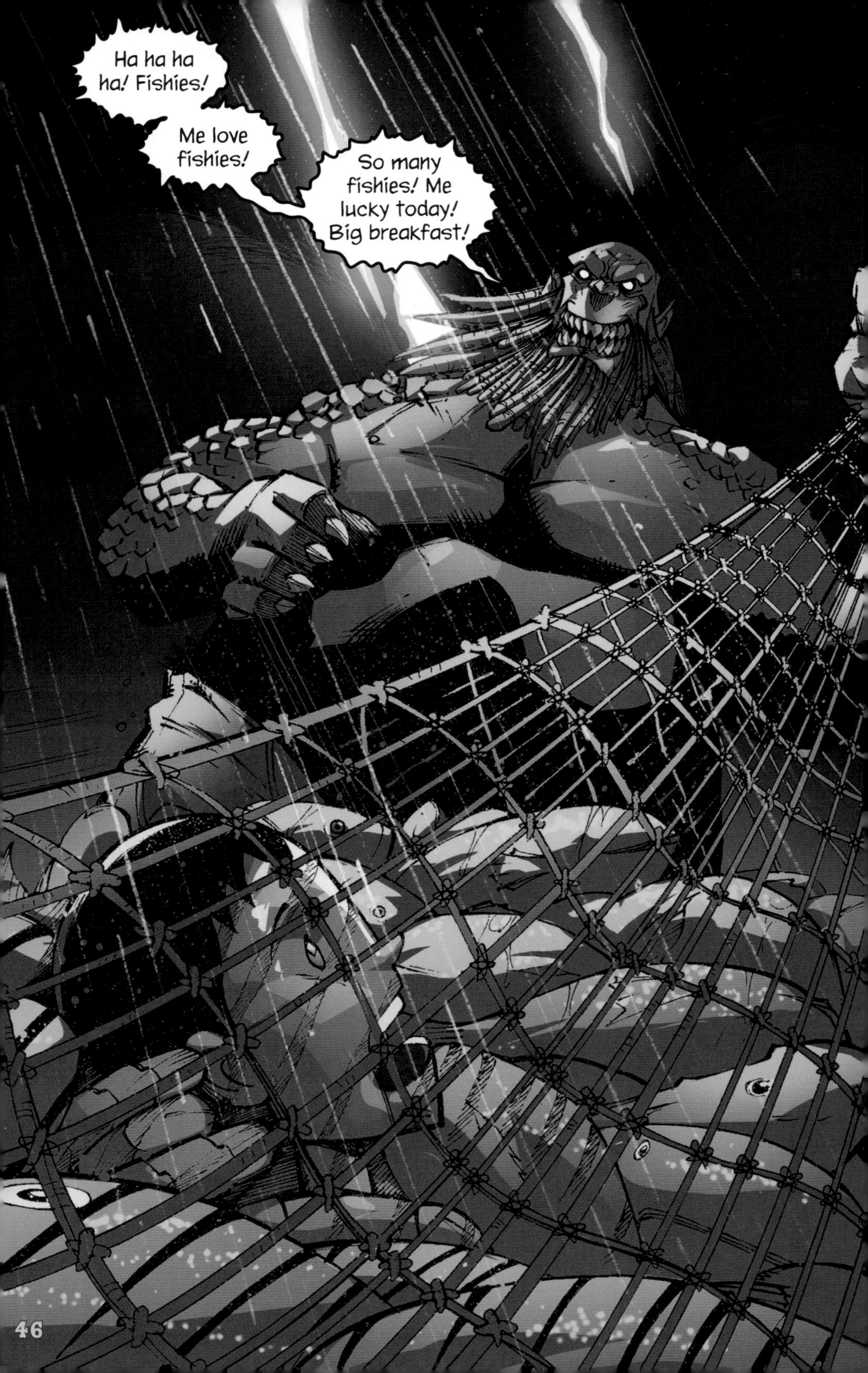
Ha ha ha ha! Fishies!
Me love fishies!
So many fishies! Me lucky today! Big breakfast!

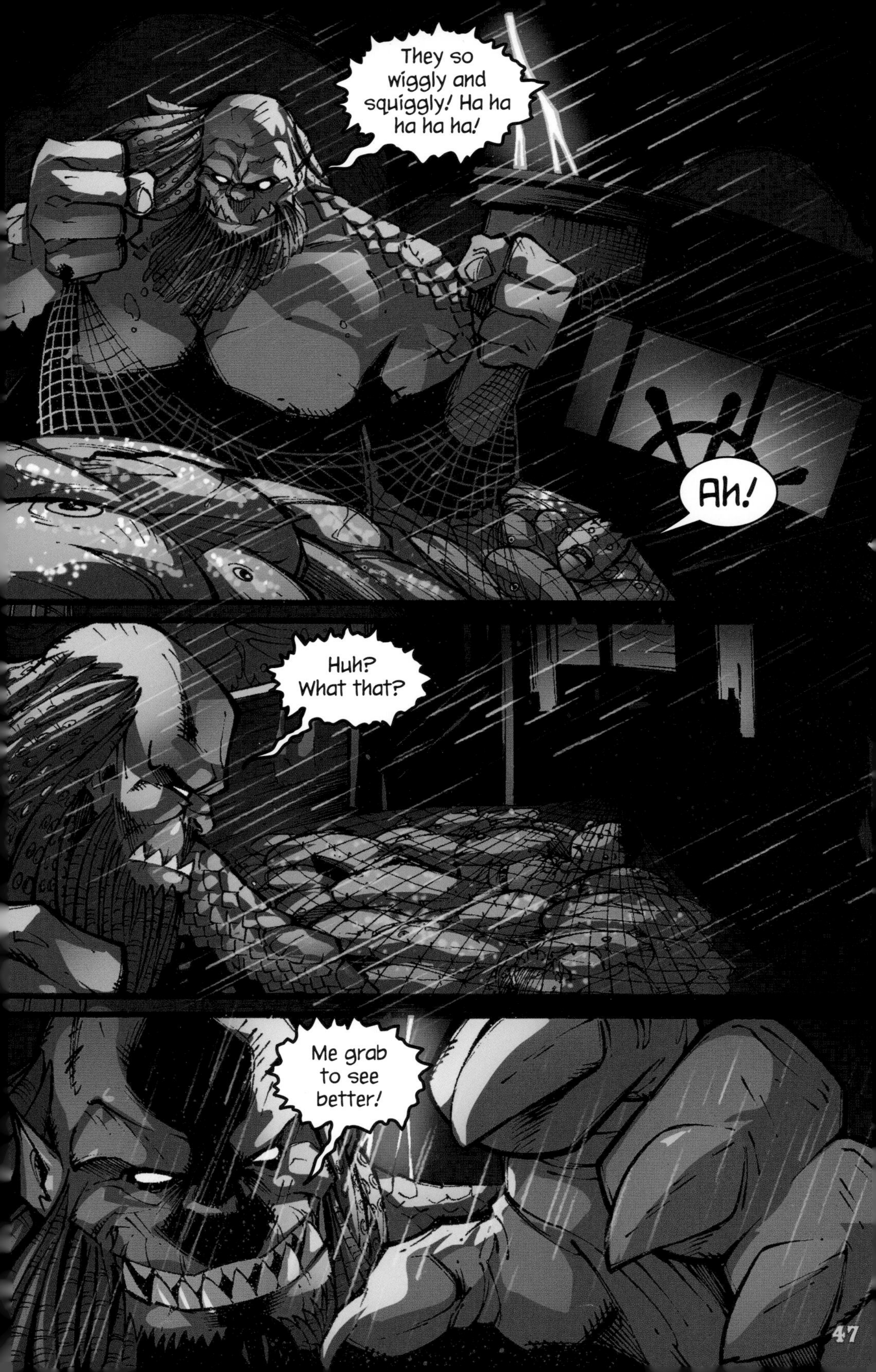
They so wiggly and squiggly! Ha ha ha ha ha!
Ah!
Huh? What that?
Me grab to see better!

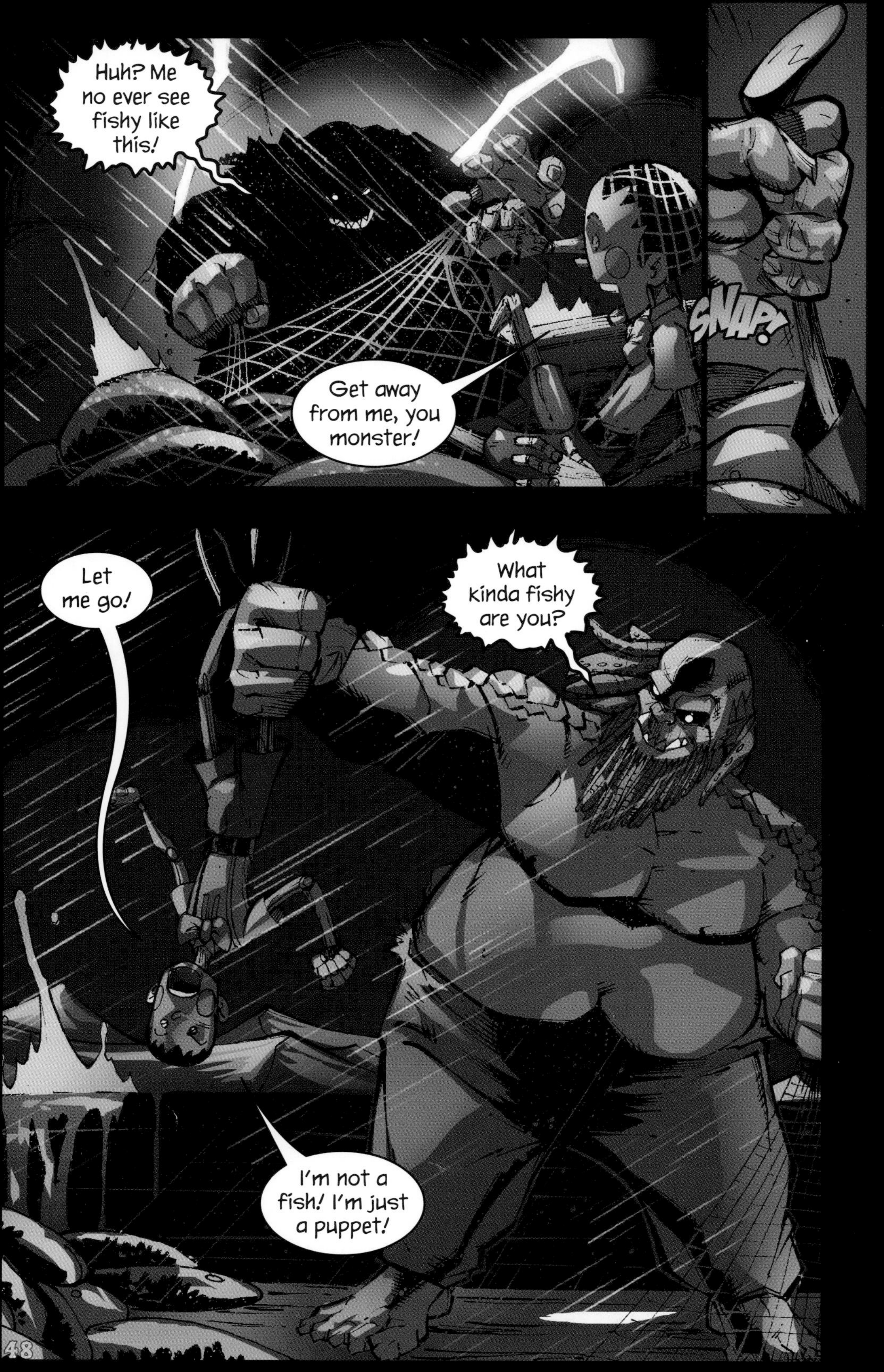
Huh? Me no ever see fishy like this!
Get away from me, you monster!
SNAP!
Let me go!
What kinda fishy are you?
I'm not a fish! I'm just a puppet!

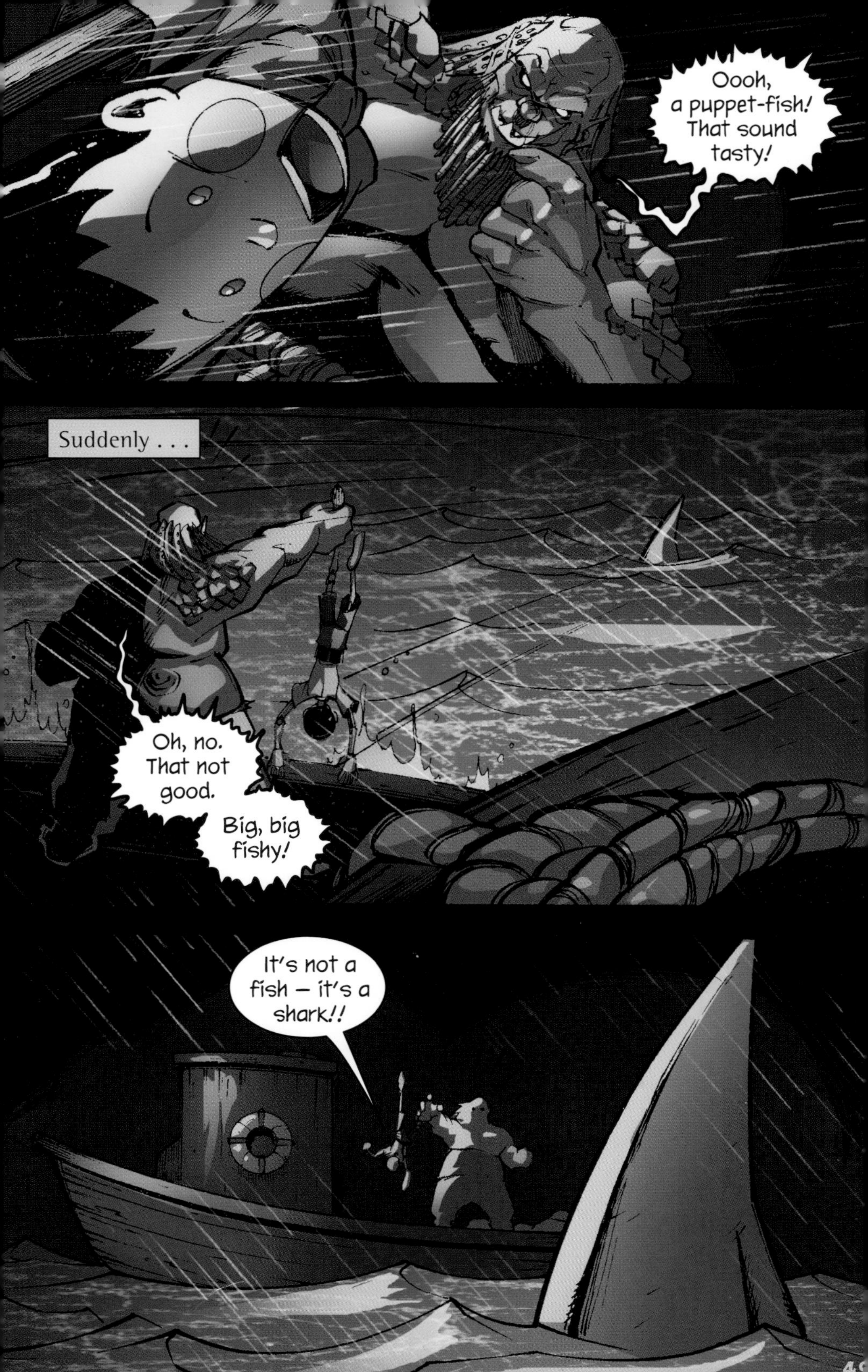
Oooh, a puppet-fish! That sound tasty!
Suddenly . . .
Oh, no. That not good.
Big, big fishy!
It's not a fish — it's a shark!!

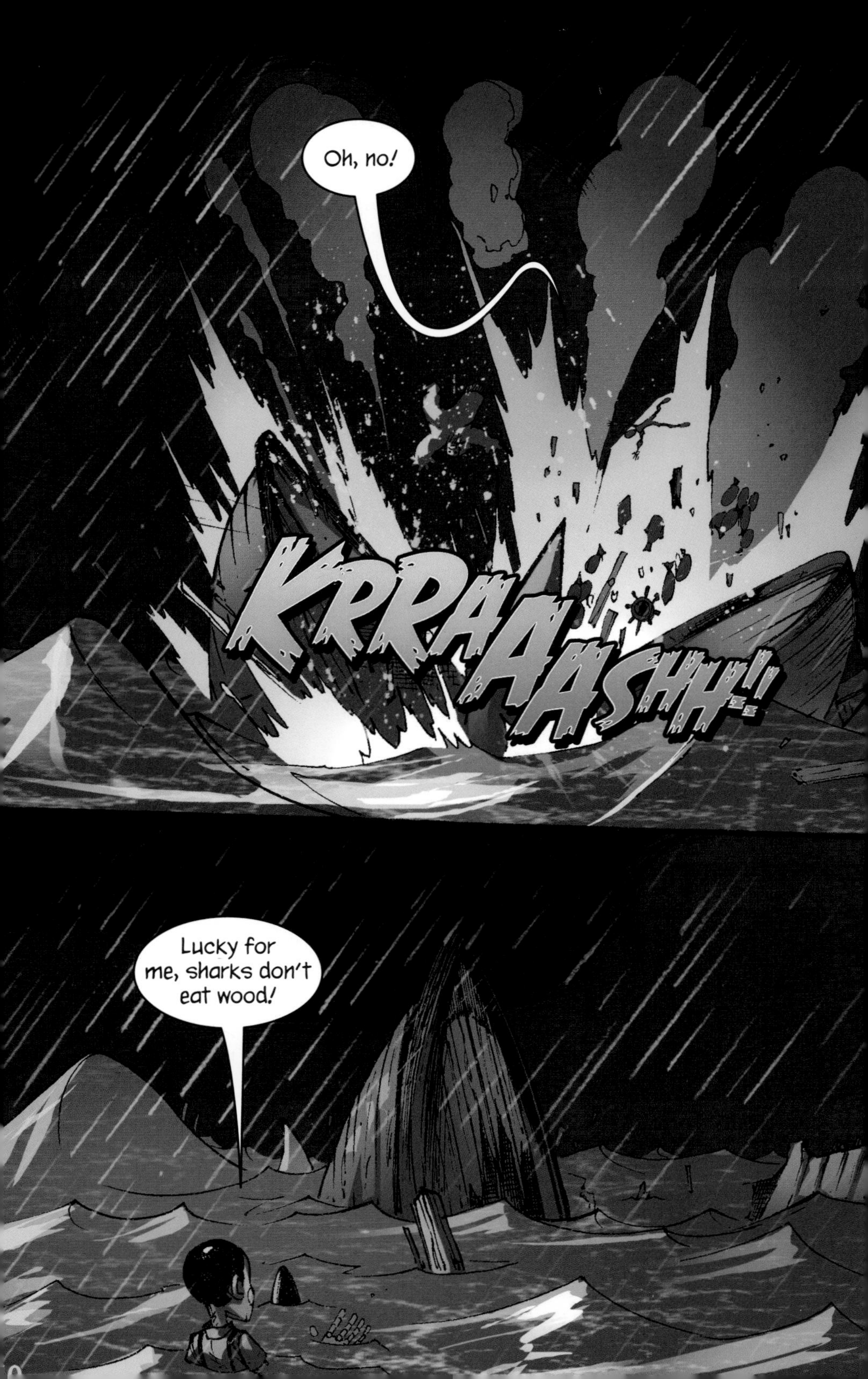
Oh, no!
KRRAAAASHH!!
Lucky for me, sharks don't eat wood!

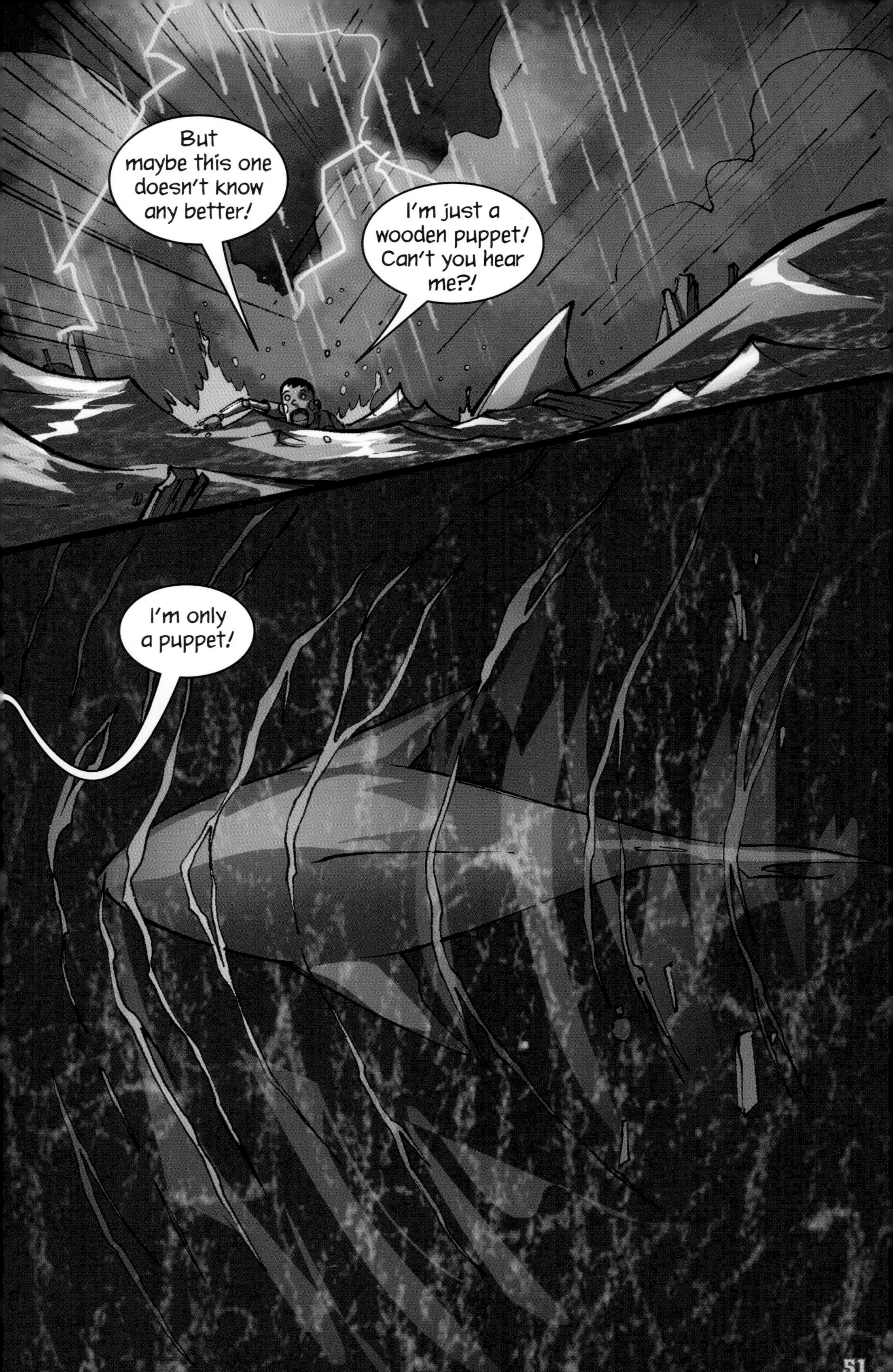
But maybe this one doesn't know any better!
I'm just a wooden puppet! Can't you hear me?!
I'm only a puppet!

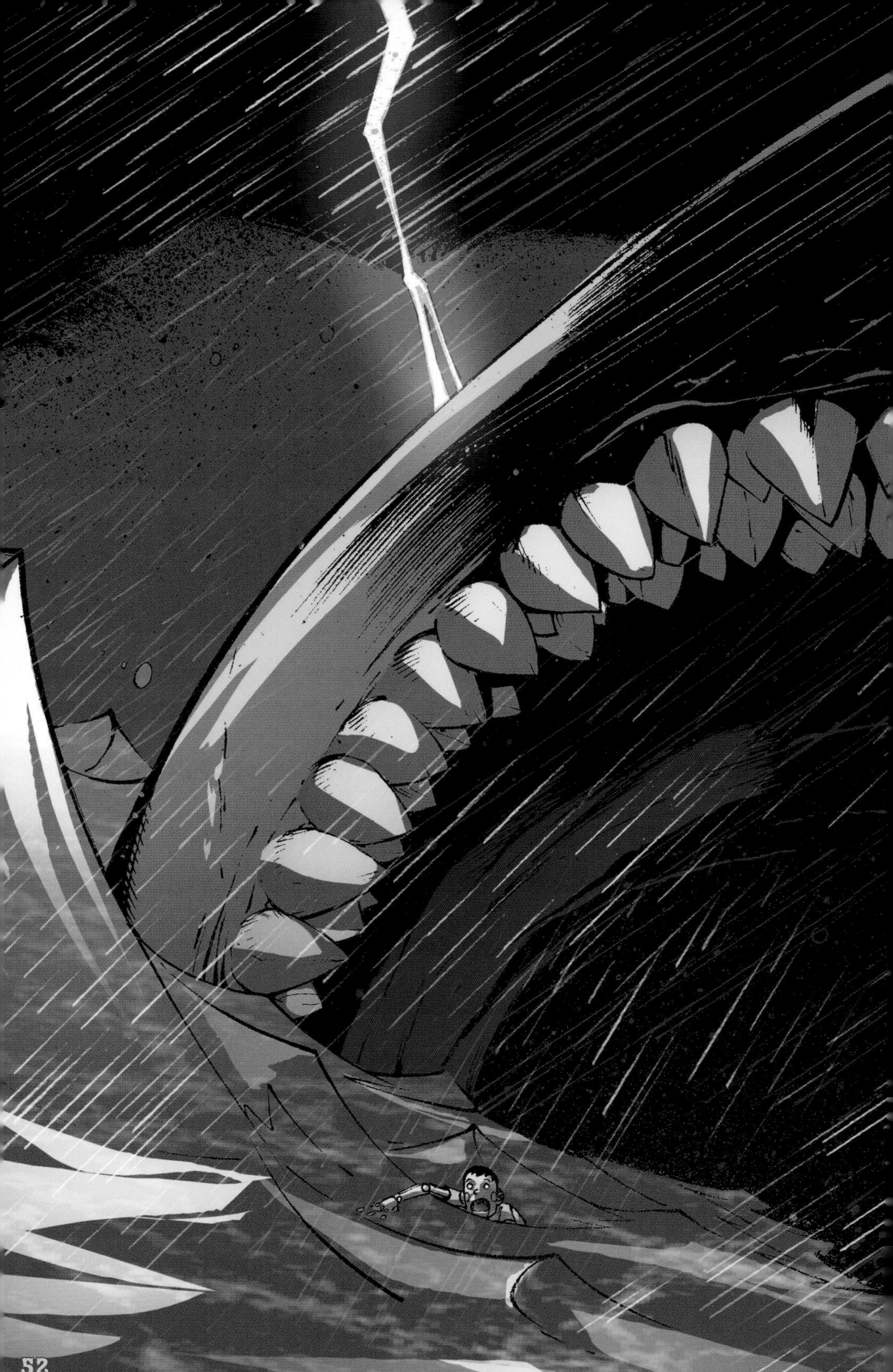

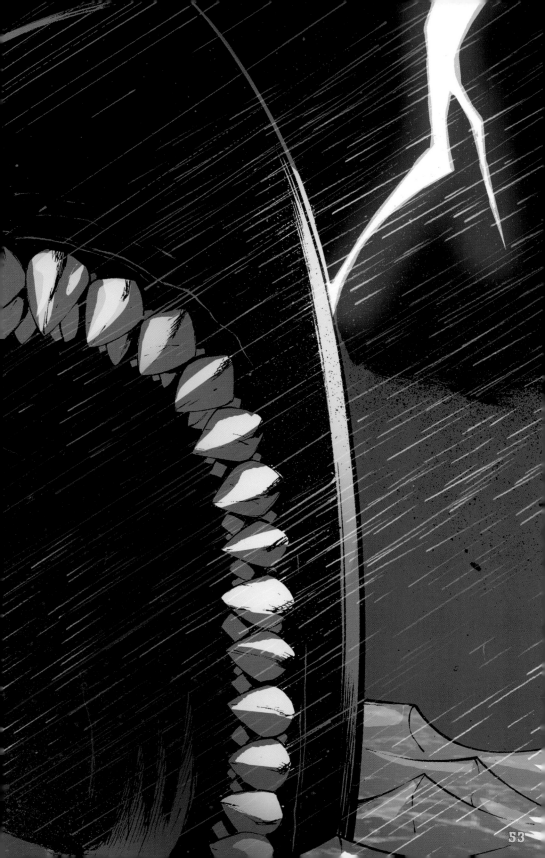

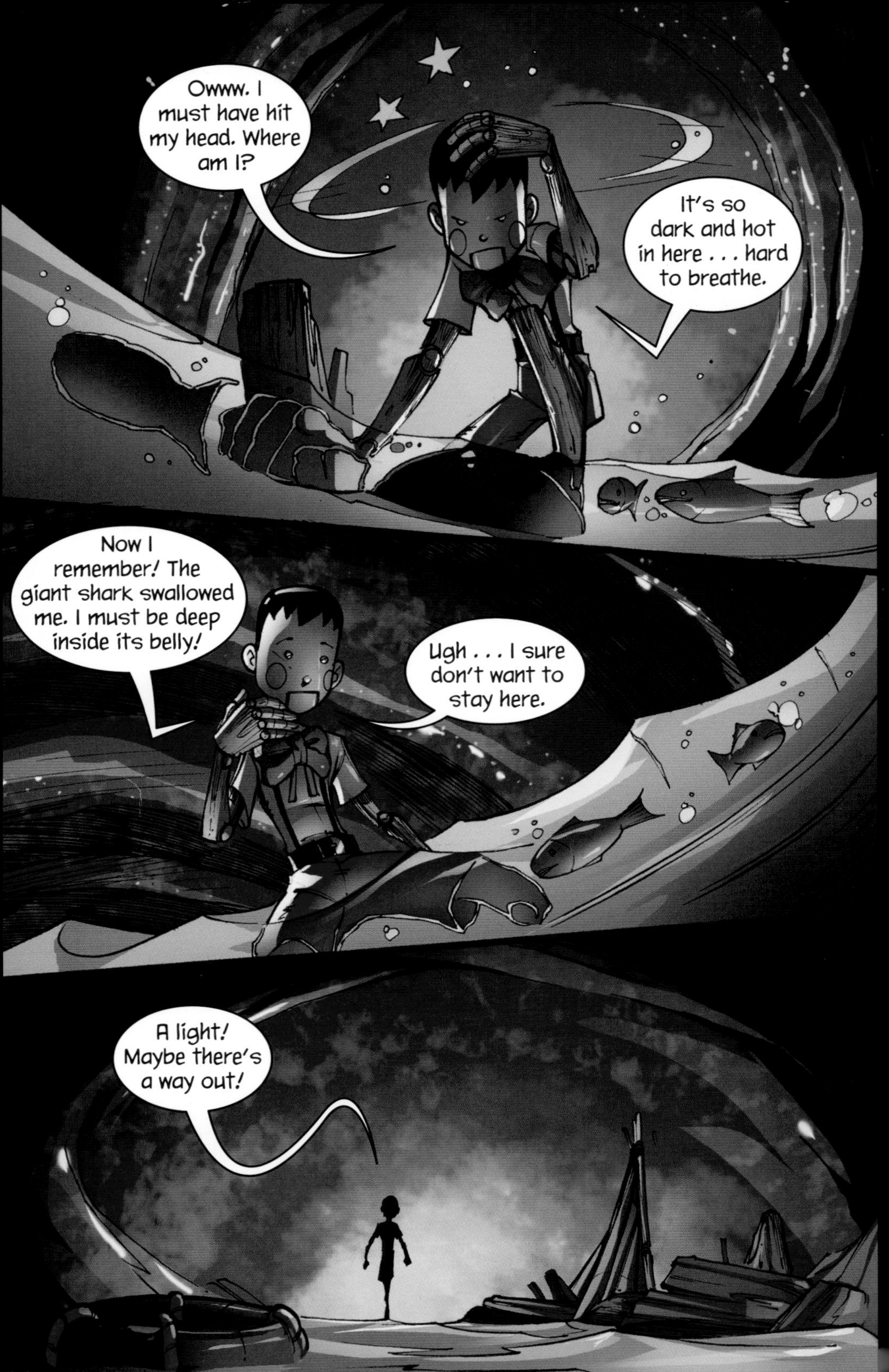
Owww. I must have hit my head. Where am I?
It's so dark and hot in here . . . hard to breathe.
Now I remember! The giant shark swallowed me. I must be deep inside its belly!
Ugh . . . I sure don't want to stay here.
A light! Maybe there's a way out!

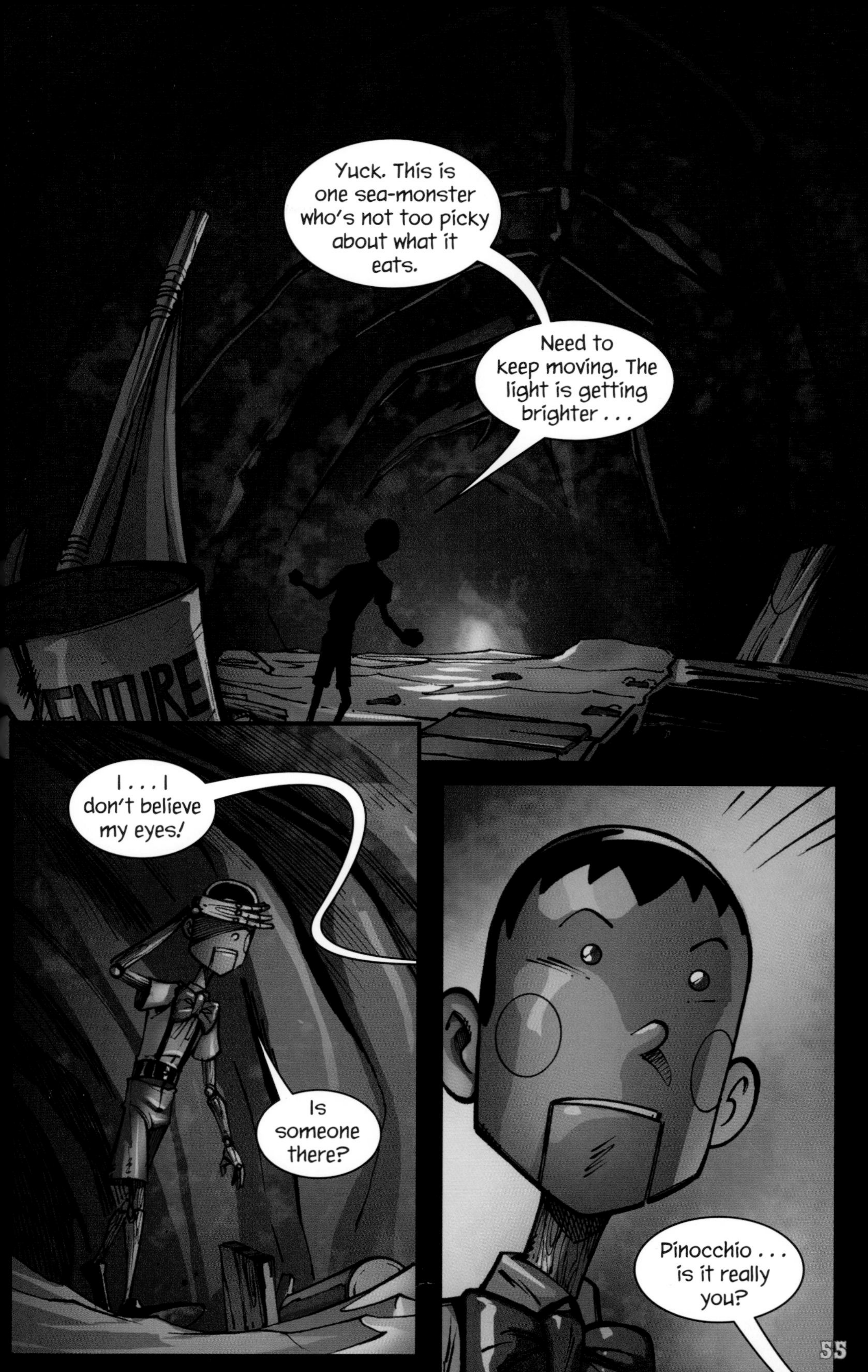
Yuck. This is one sea-monster who's not too picky about what it eats.
Need to keep moving. The light is getting brighter . . .
I . . . I don't believe my eyes!
Is someone there?
Pinocchio . . . is it really you?

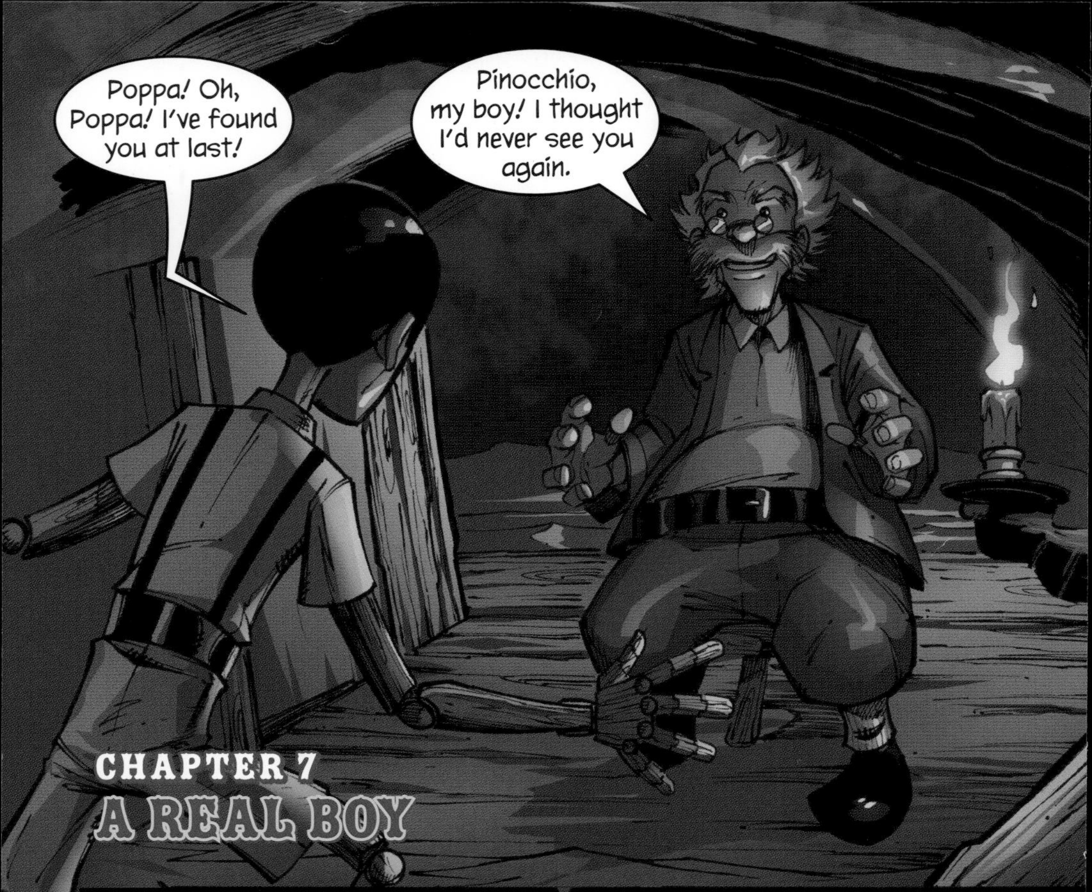

CHAPTER 7

A REAL BOY

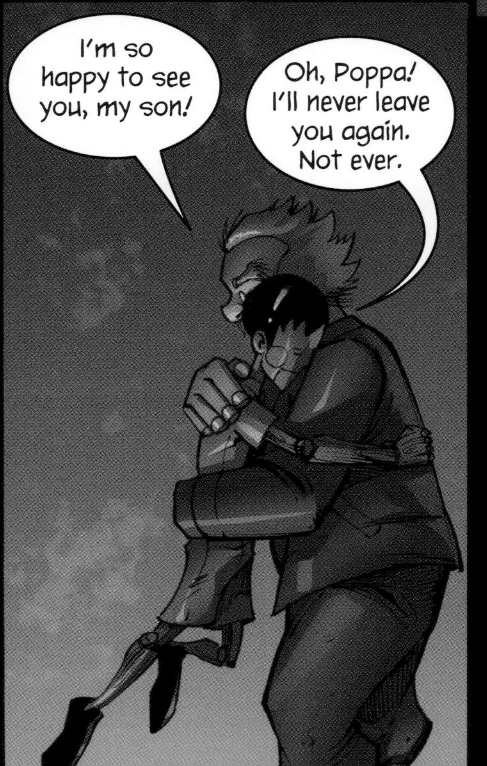

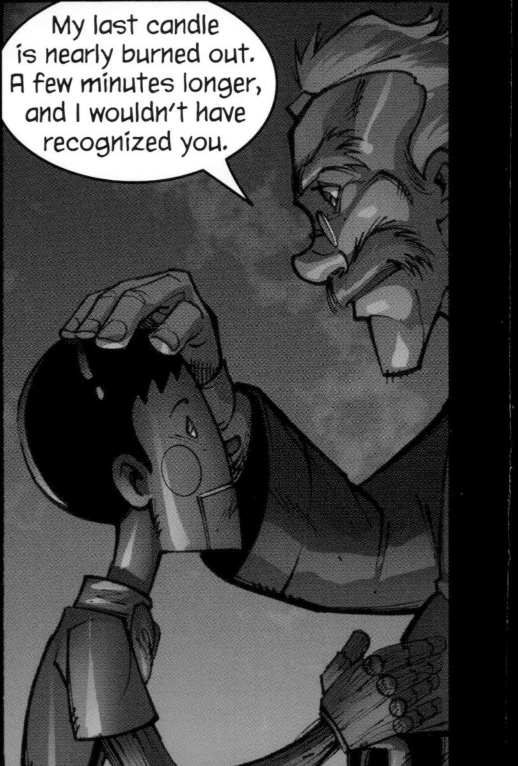

If that's the case, we have no time to lose. We must find a way to escape right now!
Escape, Pinocchio? But how?
Listen! The old shark is snoring!
Maybe we can slip out through its big mouth while it sleeps!
That sounds like a smart plan, my boy . . . but I'm afraid that I can't swim!
Don't worry, Poppa! I'm made of wood, remember?
You can float on my back!
I guess we have nothing to lose then, do we?

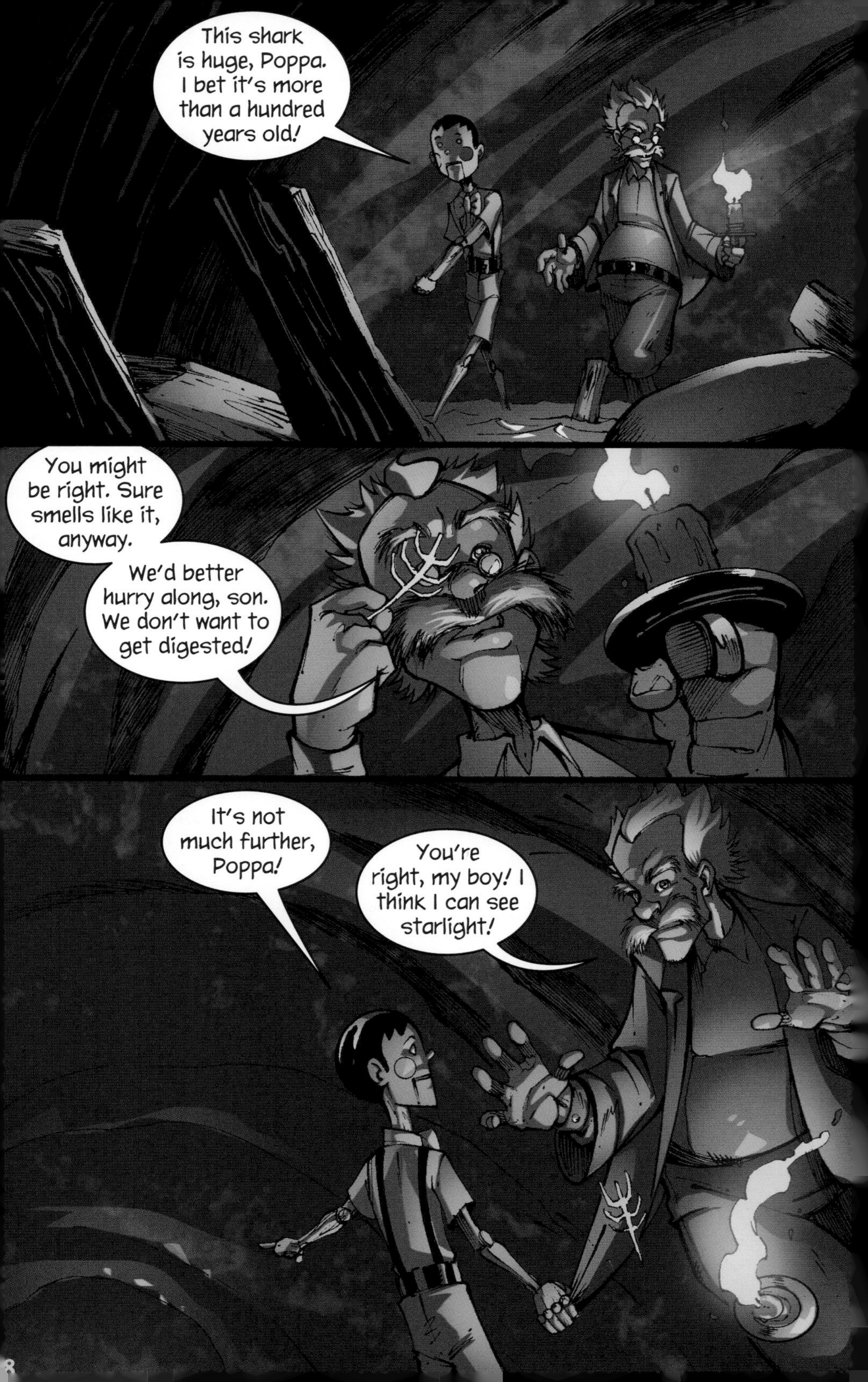

This shark is huge, Poppa. I bet it's more than a hundred years old!
You might be right. Sure smells like it, anyway.
We'd better hurry along, son. We don't want to get digested!
It's not much further, Poppa!
You're right, my boy! I think I can see starlight!

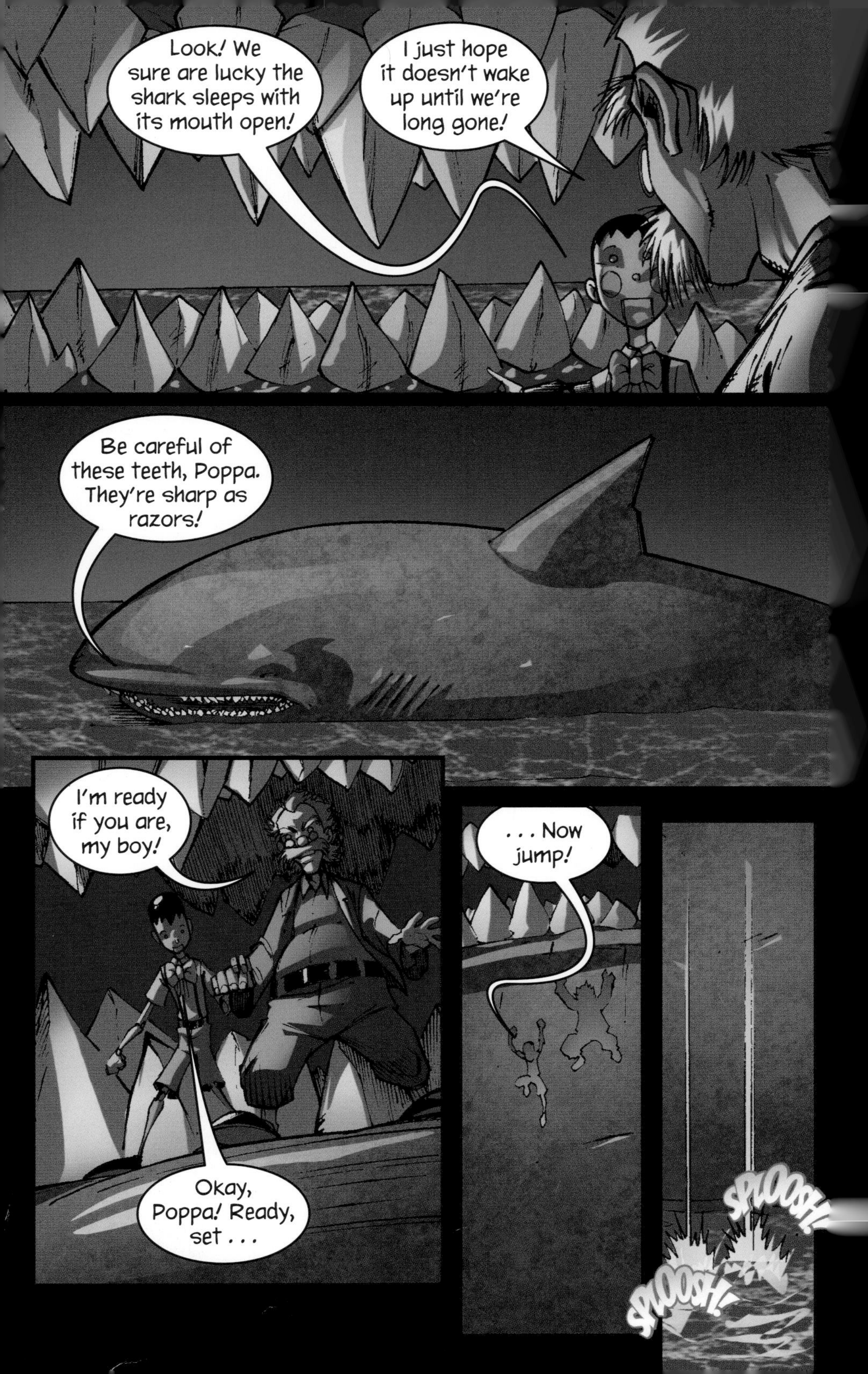
Look! We sure are lucky the shark sleeps with its mouth open!
I just hope it doesn't wake up until we're long gone!
Be careful of these teeth, Poppa. They're sharp as razors!
I'm ready if you are, my boy!
Okay, Poppa! Ready, set . . .
. . . Now jump!
SPLOOSH!
SPLOOSH!

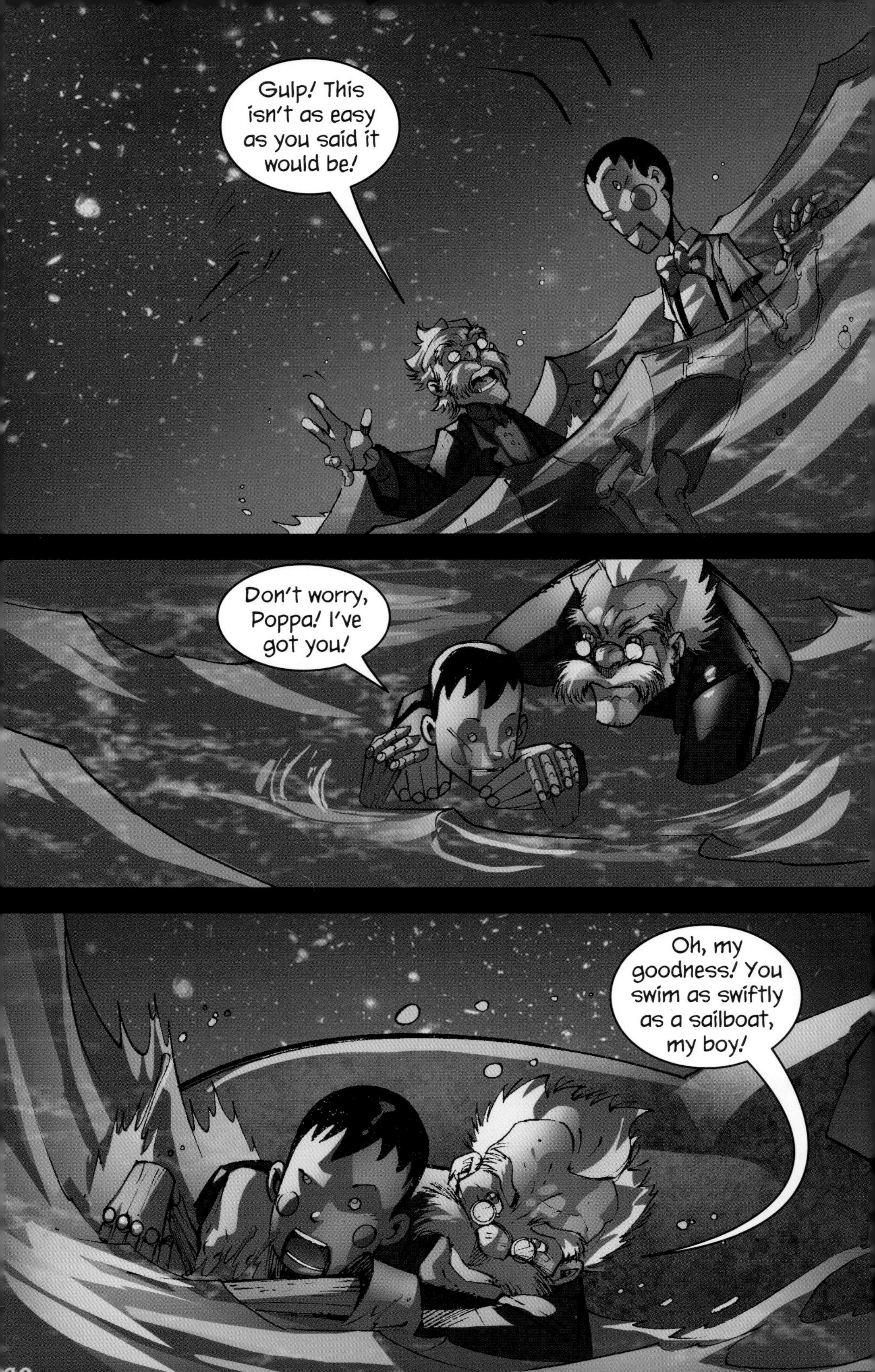
Gulp! This isn't as easy as you said it would be!
Don't worry, Poppa! I've got you!
Oh, my goodness! You swim as swiftly as a sailboat, my boy!

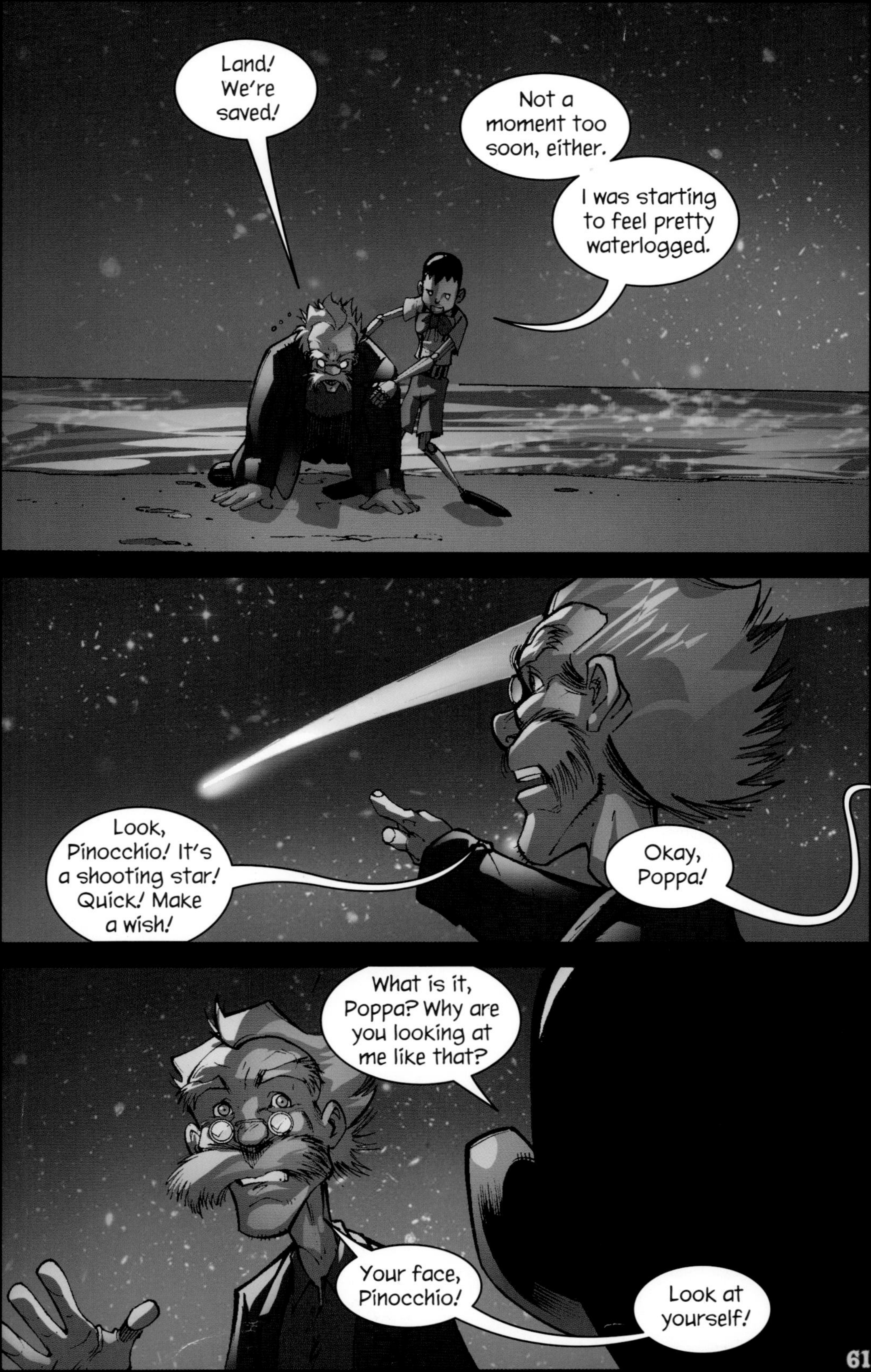
Land! We're saved!
Not a moment too soon, either.
I was starting to feel pretty waterlogged.
Look, Pinocchio! It's a shooting star! Quick! Make a wish!
Okay, Poppa!
What is it, Poppa? Why are you looking at me like that?
Your face, Pinocchio!
Look at yourself!

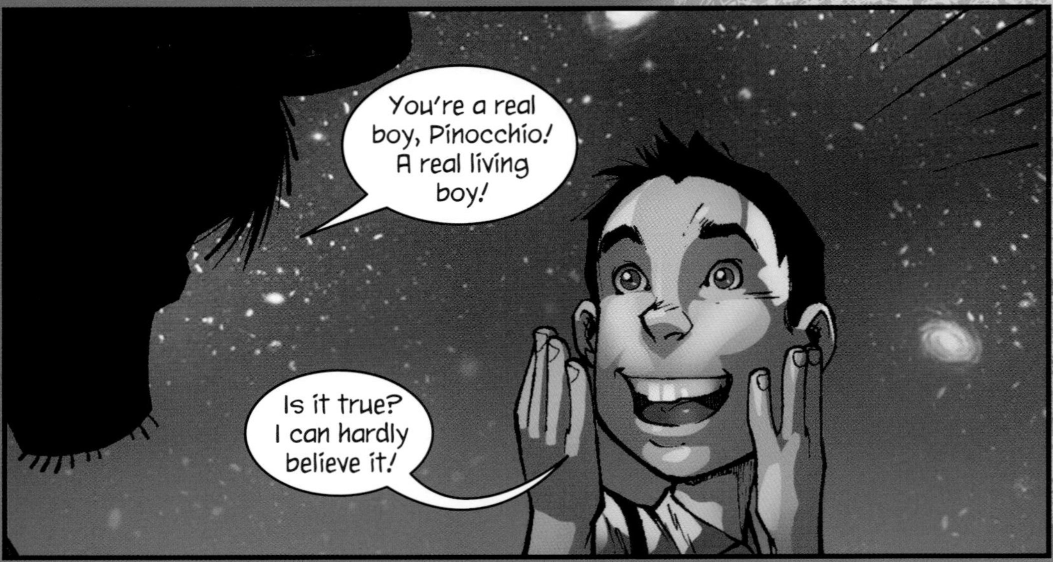
You're a real boy, Pinocchio! A real living boy!
Is it true? I can hardly believe it!

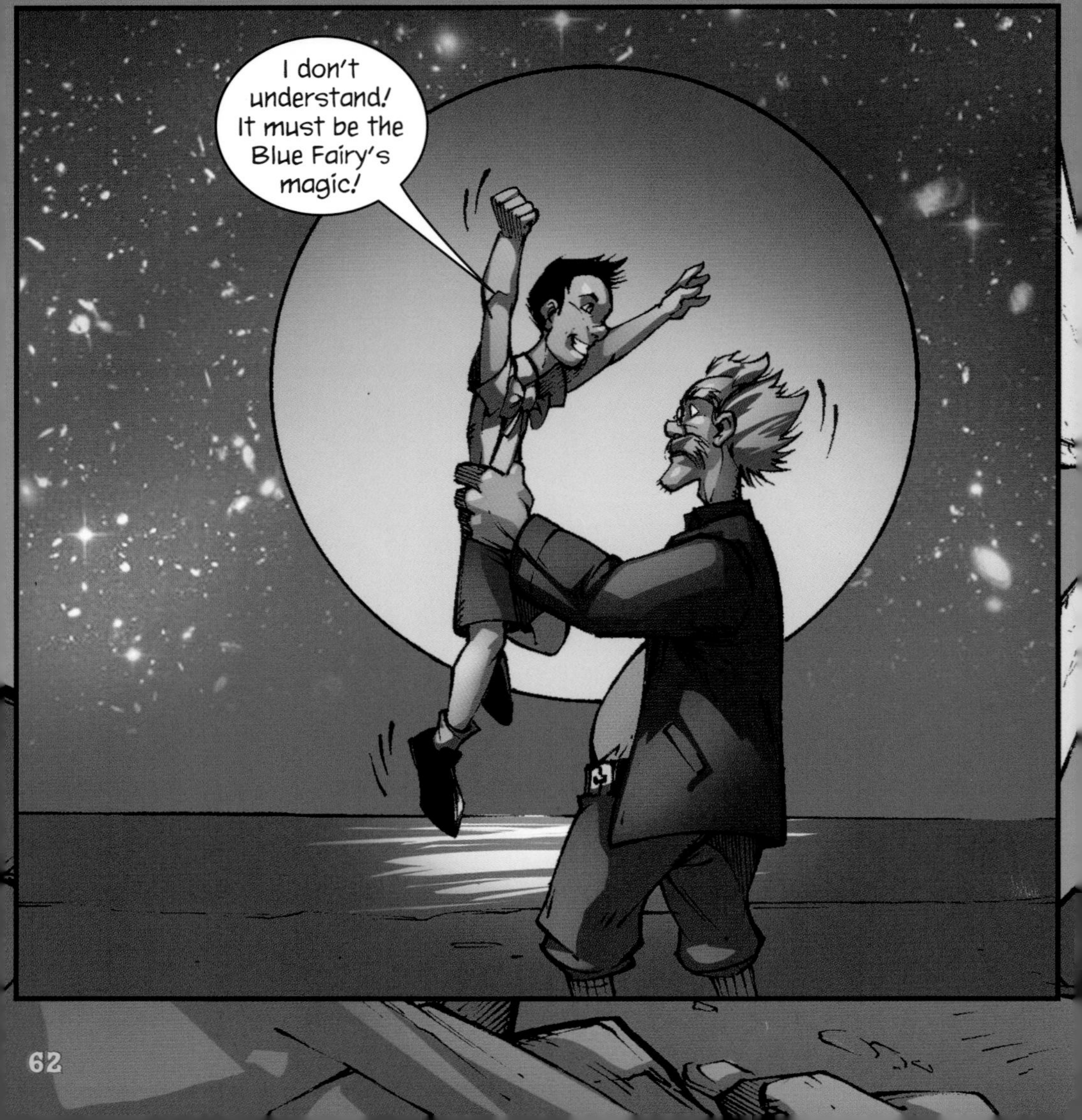
I don't understand! It must be the Blue Fairy's magic!

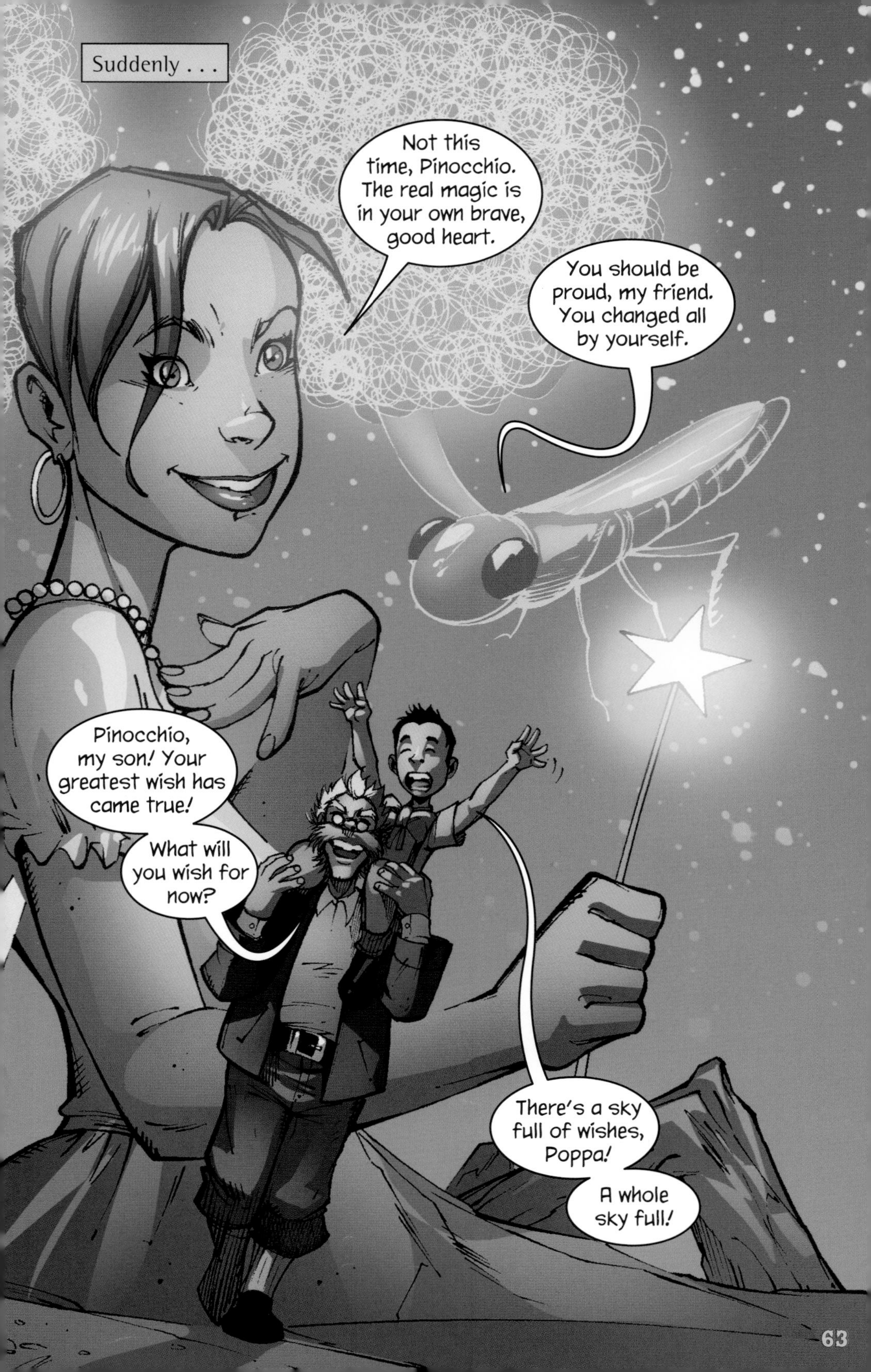
Suddenly . . .
Not this time, Pinocchio. The real magic is in your own brave, good heart.
You should be proud, my friend. You changed all by yourself.
Pinocchio, my son! Your greatest wish has came true!
What will you wish for now?
There's a sky full of wishes, Poppa!
A whole sky full!

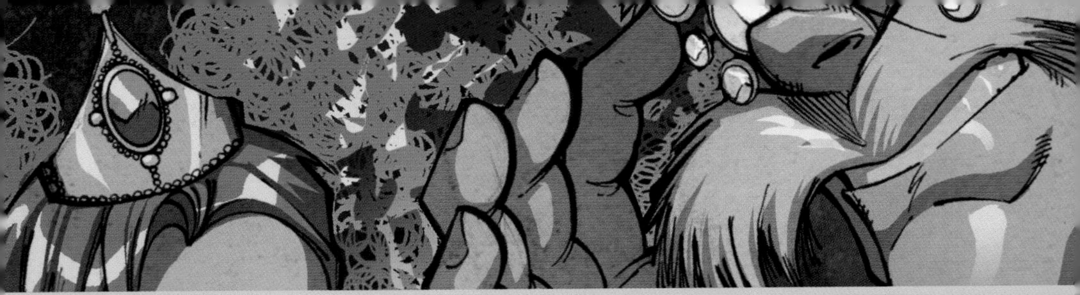

TYPES OF PUPPETS

MARIONETTES are kinds of puppets that are controlled from above using strings. These strings are usually connected to a metal or wooden rod that is held by the marionette puppeteer, or "manipulator." Marionettes are very difficult to use, because a combination of strings must be pulled to make the puppet perform simple movements.

VENTRILOQUIST DUMMIES are types of puppets that are controlled with one hand by way of a small glove attached to the puppet's back. They are called "dummies" because they can't speak – instead, the ventriloquist throws his voice and moves the dummy's mouth in sync, making it sound and look like the words are coming from the puppet's mouth.

CARNIVAL OR BODY PUPPETS are human-sized puppets that are used in parades and celebrations. One or more puppeteers move the body, arms, and legs. They are often used when the audience is far away, since they are easy to see from a distance. Big Bird from *Sesame Street* is a body puppet.

HAND PUPPETS are controlled by a single hand from inside the puppet. The puppeteer's hand controls the mouth and head, leaving the puppet's body to hang loosely over the puppeteer's arm. Other parts of the puppet, including eyelids, are often moveable as well. A sock puppet is a simplest type of hand puppet.

PUPPET TRIVIA

There is evidence that puppets were used in Egypt more than 4,000 years ago in 2,000 BC. Some historians believe puppets have even been used as far back as the year 30,000 BC!

In 1892, the great writer Oscar Wilde joked that puppets are ideal actors because "they never argue" and "they have no private lives."

Puppets were used in many royal courts to tell kings and queens bad news. Messengers, afraid of being hanged for saying something that would upset the king or queen, figured that they were less likely to be punished if the bad news was given by a puppet instead. Anything the puppet did or said could be dismissed as comedy, making it easier for a ruler to accept the bad news if it was upsetting.

In 1947, the TV show *Howdy Doody* introduced a marionette to Saturday-morning TV. The show was a big hit with children, airing until 1960.

The famous children's show *Sesame Street* began airing in 1969. It featured puppets called Muppets, which are a combination of puppets and marionettes. Big Bird and Oscar the Grouch are two of the shows most recognizable characters. *Sesame Street* episodes are still popular with kids to this day.

ABOUT THE AUTHOR

CARLO COLLODI was the pen name of Carlo Lorenzini. He was an Italian children's author who lived from November 24, 1826, to October 26, 1890. In 1880, Carlo began writing a story called "Le avventure di Pinocchio," which was published weekly in an Italian newspaper for children. In 1883, the entire collection of stories was published as a book called *The Adventures of Pinocchio.* Today, the book is considered a classic.

ABOUT THE RETELLING AUTHOR

MARTIN POWELL has been a freelance writer since 1986. He has written hundreds of stories, many of which have been published by Disney, Marvel, Tekno Comix, Moonstone Books, and others. In 1989, Powell received an Eisner Award nomination for his graphic novel *Scarlet in Gaslight.* This award is one of the highest comic book honors.

GLOSSARY

digested (dye-JEST-id)—broken down as food in the stomach

disobeying (diss-oh-BAY-ing)—going against the rules or someone's wishes

fairy (FAIR-ee)—a magical creature with wings who is often found in fairy tales

gigantic (jye-GAN-tik)—huge

grief (GREEF)—a feeling of great sadness

miracle (MEER-uh-kuhl)—an amazing event that cannot be explained by the laws of nature

recognized (REK-uhg-nized)—saw someone and knew who they were

ruined (ROO-ind)—lost wealth or was destroyed

stubborn (STUHB-urn)—not willing to give in or change

vicious (VISH-uhss)—cruel and mean, or evil and dangerous

wondrous (WUHN-druhss)—wonderful or remarkable

DISCUSSION QUESTIONS

1. Why do you think Pinocchio had such a hard time being good? Is he to blame for his mistakes, or is he innocent because he's new to the world? Discuss your answers.

2. Is it harder to be a kid or an adult? Why?

3. Each spread, or page, in a graphic novel has several panels, or illustrations. Which panel in this book is your favorite, and why?

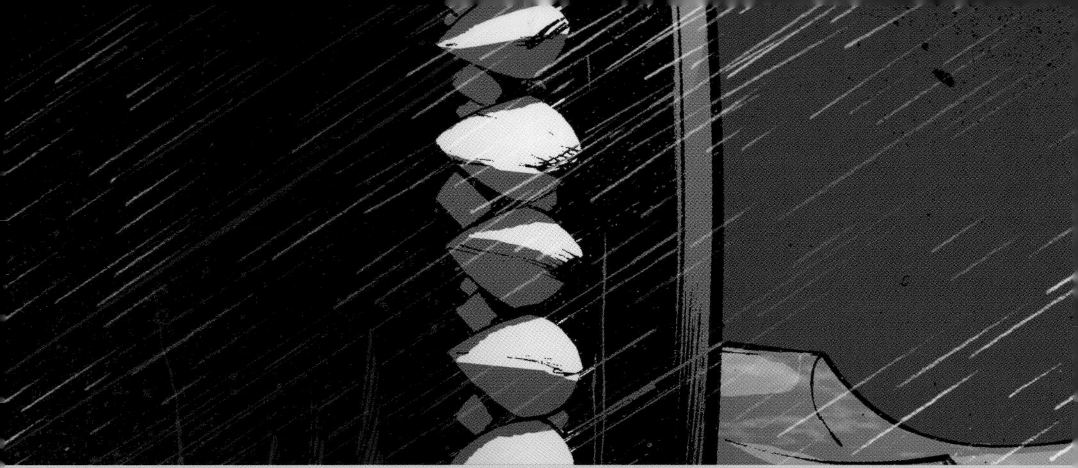

WRITING PROMPTS

1. At the end of this book, Pinocchio has become a real, living boy. Write another chapter to this book about his adventures as a real boy. Where does he go? What does he do? You decide.

2. Miss Cat and Mr. Fox tricked Pinocchio. Have you ever been tricked? What happened? How were you tricked? How did it make you feel? Write about it.

3. The monstrous fisherman who catches Pinocchio plans on eating the little wooden puppet for breakfast. If you were Pinocchio, how could you have convinced him to let you go? Write about the conversation you'd have with the monster.

STONE ARCH BOOKS

GRAPHIC NOVEL
Lewis Carroll's
Alice in Wonderland
retold by Martin Powell
illustrated by Daniel Perez
CLASSIC FICTION

GRAPHIC NOVEL
RUDYARD KIPLING'S
THE JUNGLE BOOK
CARL BOWEN
GERARDO SANDOVAL
CLASSIC FICTION

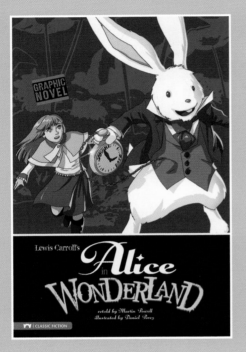

ALICE IN WONDERLAND

One day, a young girl named Alice spots a frantic White Rabbit wearing a waistcoat and carrying a pocket watch. She follows the hurried creature down a hole into the magical world of Wonderland. While there, Alice meets more crazy creatures, and plays a twisted game of croquet with the Queen of Hearts. But when the Queen turns against her, this dream-like world quickly becomes a nightmare.

THE JUNGLE BOOK

In the jungles of India, a pack of wolves discover a young boy. They name the boy Mowgli and protect him against dangers, including Shere Kan, the most savage tiger in the jungle. As Mowgli grows up, he learns the ways of the jungle from Bagheera the panther, the wise bear, Baloo, and other animals. Soon, he must decide whether to remain among beasts or embrace his own kind.

CLASSICS!

GRAPHIC NOVEL
CARLO COLLODI'S
PINOCCHIO
RETOLD BY MARTIN POWELL
ILLUSTRATED BY JOSE ALFONSO OCAMPO RUIZ
CLASSIC FICTION

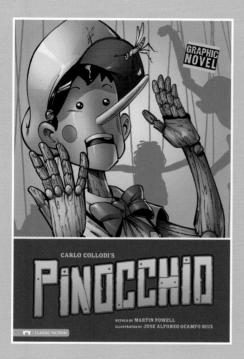

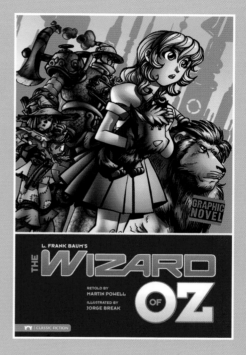

PINOCCHIO

Once upon a time, the dream of a lonely woodcutter is fulfilled when his puppet comes to life. Unfortunately, Pinocchio quickly becomes more of a prankster than a pleasure. He would rather create mischief and play tricks than keep up on his studies. Soon, however, the wooden puppet learns that being a real boy is much more complicated than simply having fun.

GRAPHIC NOVEL
L. FRANK BAUM'S
THE WIZARD OF OZ
RETOLD BY MARTIN POWELL
ILLUSTRATED BY JORGE BREAK
CLASSIC FICTION

THE WIZARD OF OZ

On a bright summer day, a cyclone suddenly sweeps across the Kansas sky. A young girl named Dorothy and her dog, Toto, are carried up into the terrible storm. Far, far away, they crash down in a strange land called Oz. To return home, Dorothy must travel to the Emerald City and meet the all-powerful Wizard of Oz. But the journey won't be easy, and she'll need the help of a few good friends.

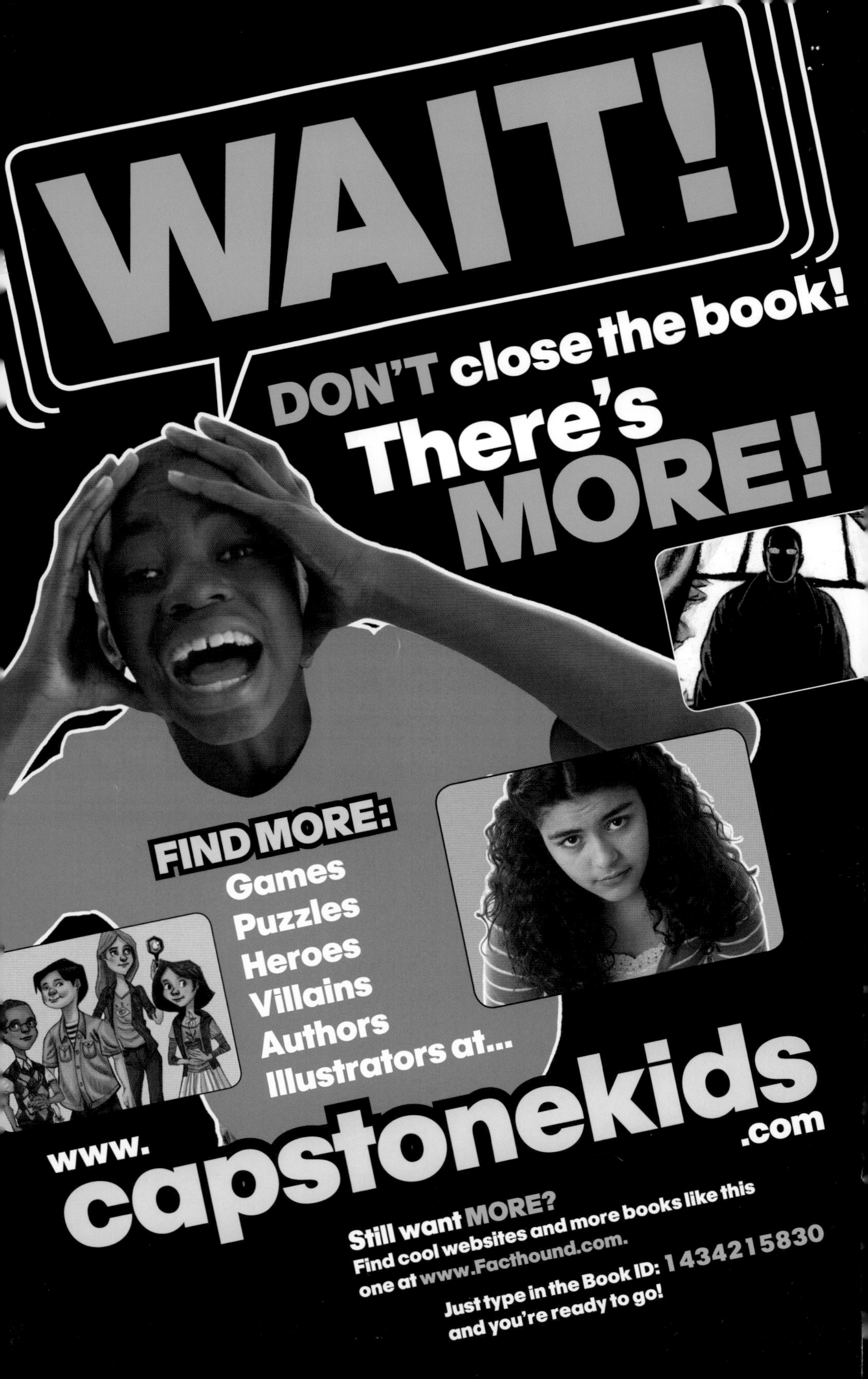
WAIT!
DON'T close the book!
There's MORE!
FIND MORE:
Games
Puzzles
Heroes
Villains
Authors
Illustrators at...
www.capstonekids.com
Still want MORE?
Find cool websites and more books like this one at www.Facthound.com.
Just type in the Book ID: 1434215830
and you're ready to go!